Kit Parker has loved writing almost as long as she's loved reading, though that took a little encouragement, and a lot of Roald Dahl, in the beginning. Since attempting her own sequel to Matilda, aged eight, she has continued to write stories with a large dollop of the fantastical.

Also being a fan of stories on screen found Kit working at a cinema during her student years and taking a writing degree in Southampton with a media twist.

She currently lives in Sussex and can often be found listening to a rather bonkers selection of music.

Also by Kit Parker:

Magical Romance
Feels Like Home

The Pool Valley Trilogy
Blood Bound
Fate Bound
Fire Bound

Coming soon:
Let it Snow

FIRE BOUND

KIT PARKER

Book three of the Pool Valley trilogy

First published in 2024 by Hellcat Publishing
Copyright © 2024 Kirsty Sian Small
Writing as Kit Parker

Kit Parker has asserted her right to be identified as the author of this work in accordance with the Copyright, Designs and Patents Act 1988

A CIP catalogue for this book is available from the British Library

ISBN: 978-1-915462-06-0

Cover design by Hellcat Publishing
Cover image courtesy of Depositphotos.com

For everyone who has waited patiently (or not).
Thank you.

The city: Pool Valley

The population: 4,623,022

Of which are human: 79

Location: Classified

LAST MARCH

Aiden sank his claws into the throat one of the last intruders, shoving him into the corner before ripping his throat out. Blood sprayed as the werewolf writhed and gurgled his way to the ground but by the time he'd hit the deck there was silence from his windpipe.

Aiden went to wipe his face of the freshly sprayed crimson but found that his clothing was already saturated in it, only a small spot on his shoulder was dry enough to get it out of his eyes and mouth. Rubbing his face as best he could with the raised shoulder, one arm above his head, he turned back to the blood bath behind him.

Rogue and pack werewolves lay intertwined in broken heaps across the floor, it was difficult to identify many of them for the sheer amount of blood. Others may just as well have fallen asleep on mounds of the innards of others. Aiden flinched at the sight of Lucy, their youngest female member, or what was left of her. His stomach rolled at the horror her attacker had subjected her teenage body to. Seventeen was no age at all.

'I think she died almost instantly, if that's any consolation.' Acheron lay a hand on his son's shoulder. 'I can't say the same for some of our number,' he said, flinching as a gun fired and the moaning Aiden had been trying to tune out ceased.

They both looked up in time to see Danyl lowering the handgun they kept in the office, Seth limping up behind him.

Aiden turned a full three-sixty, taking in the carnage.

Kia and Nick, with Oakley and Ramsey's help were beginning to sift through the bodies, separating out the pack members from the rogues. Nick was shovelling any intruders they found out onto the patio, throwing them one by one into a growing pile.

'How did this happen?' Aiden turned to his father. He'd been alpha less than a year, he hadn't had time to make enemies.

'I have my suspicions, but let's not speculate for now. They were some thirty strong when they hit, but judging by the bodies in here, I'd say some retreated before we could wipe them out.'

'That means whoever it was will be back.'

'They probably think that with a new alpha in situ, we might have weakened. We were caught unawares, but we're still here.'

'Someone with a grudge?' Aiden placed his hands on his hips as his eyes slid back to his father.

'I ousted a wolf called Cain when I found out Sookie was carrying you. I had been watching his behaviour for some time and didn't like what I saw. As expected, when asked to leave he challenged me for the pack, and I refused to acknowledge it. I made a choice I believed was for the best for my family.' Acheron shrugged. 'He could have attempted to take it from me there and then, but he didn't. I assumed he'd chosen to become a lone wolf. He didn't approach the O'Neill pack.'

'We need to find him. Quickly.'

'I agree.'

'If it is Cain, is he calculated enough to wait for a moment like this?'

'It would seem so. He also didn't make an appearance in person, which would suggest that this was research or damage maximisation.' Acheron slapped Aiden on the back gently and moved off into the centre of the room where surviving pack members were laying out their dead and preparing to grieve. Most of them were still too shocked to process what had happened.

Aiden stepped over to the patio doors where Kia, Oakley and Ramsey were laying out the last of the attackers.

'Don't burn them yet.' He looked to Kia. 'I want pictures, especially identifying marks. We need to know who they were and who sent them.'

Kia nodded and looked to Nick.

'You two are fast becoming a powerhouse of destruction. I think that could have been even more deadly if you hadn't been here,' Aiden addressed his brother.

It was Nick's turn to nod. 'We'll find them. No one attacks this pack and gets away with it.'

'What made you two come home?' Oakley asked. He was stood behind Ramsey, his arms wrapped around him as he wept. Oakley kissed the back of Ramsey's head, burying his nose into his lover's curly blond hair.

'It's a Friday night, college was done for the day and Kia doesn't have dance practice this weekend, so we thought we'd come and spend some time out in the garden now that the weather is on the turn.' Nick looked out at the garden, it was twilight, but he could see the March flowers springing up next to the wall and in his mother's planters.

Kia reached out and took Ramsey's hand to give it a squeeze. She reached out next to hug Aiden, but as they both took in the state of their clothing, thought better of it.

'I'm sorry we couldn't do more,' she said softly and with a glance at Nick left to look for Sookie, who had been bundled into a safe place by Acheron.

Aiden and Nick began the gruelling task of helping the rest of the pack identify who was still standing and checking the dead attackers for ID.

'How did they get in?' Nick asked his brother as they tossed the last rogue from the house together. He and Kia had arrived shortly after they'd broken in to find a number of casualties already mounting.

'From all sides. I don't think there's a ground floor window left intact.' Aiden gestured down the house in the fading light.

'Do you think they knew there was as wolves-only meeting happening this weekend?' Nick asked.

'What makes you say that?' Aiden looked up sharply.

'Why attack a pack, with clear intent of doing this kind of damage, without a *full* pack in attendance?' Nick looked at him pointedly. 'I wasn't supposed to be here.'

'More chance to take me or dad out I suppose.' Aiden shrugged even as he folded his arms.'

ONE

Kieran followed Lorna and Nick as they walked straight through the door of the restaurant without pausing, passing a flummoxed maître d', who jumped back as soon as she realised they weren't there to book a table. Lorna grinned at her as she flustered, smoothing down her white-blonde pixie cut in an attempt to look calm.

With Lorna up front, they headed straight for the back of the restaurant where the manager and a bartender stepped in front of them. Stopping abruptly Lorna felt the eyes of the whole restaurant on them.

'You can't just barge in here!' the manager exclaimed. 'We're fully booked . . . this is a respectful establishment.'

'We have reason to believe otherwise,' Lorna stated, unflinching.

'You're not the head guardian anymore, we don't have to stand back and let you trash the joint.'

'If you need her, she's outside, and who said I was here to trash the joint?' Lorna pouted but didn't wait for his response. 'Head guardian I may not be, but guardian I am, and I have business here.'

'There is no trouble here,' the manager insisted but Lorna noticed a second bartender looking skittish behind the counter.

'Oh, I don't know, some of your staff seem a bit edgy.' Lorna glanced at the bartender as he growled in return and made a break for the back room.

Nick took a step to his right, reached across the bar, and grabbed the wolf by the head, tearing it off and throwing it over his shoulder. The head, complete with surprised expression, landed in a bowl of soup hair-first, the bloody severed neck pointed directly at the punter, whose spoon was still in his mouth.

It took two seconds of silence before panic erupted as someone screamed.

The diner, whose soup was ruined, simply stared at the new addition to his starter, unsure what to do next.

'I'd say he knew something you didn't.' Nick wiped his hands clean on a napkin from the bar as he continued, his voice dangerously low. 'That or you're a better actor. Now get out.'

In an instant the clientele were on their feet and, joined by other members of staff, began making for the exits.

'Do you even know who owns this place?' the manager asked, a smug glint in his eyes as he looked each of the Barnes pack members up and down in turn. 'You have no idea who you're messing with.'

'Owned,' Lorna replied, a wicked smile in her eyes. 'It seems Angelo had been running with the wrong crowd of late, he's in the hands of the Registry.'

'We'll . . .'

'It wasn't pack business, you'll do nothing,' Nick threatened as he stepped around Lorna.

'You just made it pack business, and aren't you supposed to be dead?'

'So they keep telling me.' Nick grinned as he advanced on the manager.

His head landed moments later next to the bartender's, smacking the diner on the shoulder, causing him to drop the first head back into his soup, which he had been sniffing closely, in mind to eating. Looking up unashamedly he realised that the rest of the diners had cleared out and that the three newcomers were looking at him quizzically.

'Alright, alright, I'm going,' he grouched, throwing his napkin down as he got up.

Kieran arched an eyebrow as the creature fidgeted on the spot, glancing between them and the heads on the table. Eventually deciding it wasn't going to be a meal totally wasted, he snatched up both heads by the hair and scurried away as fast as his legs would take him.

With the room cleared, Lorna turned to Nick and her brother.

'Waste not, want not I suppose.' Lorna shrugged.

Kieran screwed his face up.

'Service!'

The cry from the serving hatch caught them all unawares.

'What the f–'

The chef was leaning out over the food, peering at the deserted tables, some of the chairs had been knocked over in the evacuation.

'Fuckit,' Lorna hissed and triggered the nearest fire alarm.

'I wonder what the special was tonight,' Nick said as the kitchen staff began filing out of a fire exit at the back of the building, he was watching them through the hatch, there were several plates of food on the warmer.

'We're not here to eat!' Lorna whirled on him and found him grinning.

'Maybe we should have asked that other guy to share?' he teased.

'Funny,' she deadpanned. 'Come on, we're now against the clock. We should assume that all staff are Cain's pack members.'

'Wait,' Nick said quickly as Lorna reached for the key-coded door marked "Staff Only". It had a circular glass panel, through which they could see the door to the kitchen.

Lorna paused and realised that she could hear heavy footfall running up a flight of stairs.

'The basement?' she whispered.

Kieran grabbed her by the arm, and they dived behind the bar as a face appeared at the door.

Biting her lip, Lorna threw a ball of fire up and over the counter as a bleeping at the door signalled that the werewolf was coming out.

The werewolf threw the door open, ready to ask someone what the hell was going on, but entered the dining room slowly, his boots thudding across the expensive hard-wood floor. He took in the lack of patrons and the table full of food now well alight in front of the bar, next to which lay the headless corpse of the manager, and growled.

Turning on his heel he headed back to the door and found it wedged open, Nick stood in front of it.

The wolf opened his mouth to yell out a warning, but Lorna appeared from behind the bar, shooting him in the side of the head before he could squeak.

'Breach! Breach!'

Nick whirled in time to see a second werewolf heading back down the stairs to the basement.

'Fuck!' Lorna jumped the bar and threw a telekinetic firebomb in his direction, barely missing Nick as he dove out of the way. 'Get after him!' she yelled at Nick even though he was already moving.

Nick started down the stairwell at the same time the sound of automatic gunfire ripped through the cellar. Pulling his sister back, Kieran shoved past the pair of them and throwing his shield up, headed down the stairs first.

Bullets sprayed up the stairs in random bursts, the sound interlaced with screams of terror and pain.

The twins advanced, doubling their shields by merging them together, Nick bringing up the rear. When basement came into view, the shooting stopped as the eight gunmen held them in their sights. Racks upon racks of food and equipment were behind them, bloody footprints covering the floor.

'Our turn now?' Lorna cooed.

As a few of the wolves began laughing, only one spoke.

'You're not coming in here. It's too late for them anyway,' he said, jerking his head to his left with a snigger.

'I beg to differ,' Lorna cooed as all their guns fell apart.

As they stepped back in confusion, Lorna stepped aside and they dropped the shield to let Nick through.

Nick wasted no time at all in grabbing the nearest head to him, wrenching it from the neck it lived on and lobbing it through the racks of stock, sending two shelving units crashing to the ground with the clatter of metal on tiles. Once Nick had the party started, the twins also waded in.

Letting his sister do pack work, Kieran threw a ball of fire at the wolf nearest to where he suspected the trafficked creatures were, slipping past as the wolf's clothes ignited and his nearest comrade attempted to put him out.

Following the bloody footprints to an office in the corner of the basement, Kieran was acutely aware of the silence beyond.

The smell of blood hit his nose long before he reached the door to the office. His head swam with the anxious feeling of failure.

As he rounded the door, he was thankful Lorna hadn't found the scene first, the one third vampire in her would have reacted to the sheer about of blood. The smell alone would have been torturous. He lifted his sleeve to his nose, hoping to abate the copper tang infecting his sinuses.

He could tell it was as Kia and Ashlie had feared, another group of female supernatural beings. They had been huddled together in the corner for comfort in a futile attempt to stick together against their captors.

Kieran ran his free hand through his hair, grabbing a fistful and tugging at the roots to distract from the horror before him.

After a steadying moment, he tried to count just how many bodies he was looking at. It wasn't easy, limbs and clothing merged in a mass of crimson.

Having managed to count twenty, Kieran was stood in the middle of the room when Lorna and Nick found him moments later, staring at an open, unseeing pair of eyes in the middle of the group, transfixed by the sadness and resignation he found there as pain had given way to death.

'Are you ok?' Lorna asked as she approached him, laying her hands on his shoulders.

'They were dead as soon as we found out where they were,' he said, his voice hollow.

'Help us,' a small, exhausted voice muttered from the back of the group. 'Please?'

They all peered into the carnage and found movement towards the back wall, the bodies in front two-deep, trapping her against a filing cabinet.

Diving forwards they began gently moving the girls around her to one side. As he worked, Nick scanned their faces for recognition.

The voice belonged to a blonde girl right at the back. When they reached her, they found her clinging onto a brunette.

'I think she's still alive, you need to help her,' she muttered through tears of shock and relief, looking from the nearest body to the girl in her arms, as they lay the girl who had been trapping her legs to one side.

'Give her to me,' Kieran asked gently, tugging the girl forwards, his focus on the living to prevent from seeing more of the dead.

As the girl fell forwards onto his shoulder, he heard her wheezing and knew that she was still with them. Turning he looked for a place to lay her down and finding only the desk, telekinetically cleared it.

'Can you help her?' Lorna glanced over as she and Nick helped the other survivor to her feet.

'I'm a bit limited down here, but I might be able to stabilise her long enough to get her to either HQ or the main hospital,' Kieran said as he inspected the bullet wound she had taken to the chest.

'Her name's Melody,' the woman Lorna was supporting mumbled.

'Do you know what Melody is?' Kieran asked gently.

'Shifter I think, some kind of canine.'

'That's useful, her own healing mechanism will be giving her the best possible chance, thank you.' Kieran offered a reassuring smile as he picked Melody up.

'What's your name?' Lorna asked. 'Were you shot anywhere else?'

'I'm Anna, I was shielded by the others–' she stopped as shock caused her whole body to shake and she choked on a sob. 'Anywhere *else*? I don't think I was.'

'It looks like it's just your shoulder,' Lorna offered. 'That and a wrenched knee.'

'Are they all dead?' she sobbed.

No one was sure whether she meant her captors or the other women. It was essentially the same question. Nick nodded silently when her eyes fell on him.

'There are other traffickers, I don't know where they are but I'm sure they said they'd be back later,' Anna said as she leant heavily on Lorna and they began shuffling towards the door.

'It's OK, we're going to get you out of here right now, there are people waiting outside to get you to safety,' Nick soothed.

'Let's move before we have any more company,' Kieran muttered, nodding, and lead them from the office, back towards the stairs.

Picking their way carefully through the bodies, Nick looked around at the carnage he'd left behind, the blood, the body parts, the trashed fixtures and fittings. Almost slipping on what turned out to be an eyeball, he looked down to see the severed head the eye had once belonged to. He'd thrown it so hard that the eye had popped out, still attached to the optic nerve.

Lorna glanced back to see the look on his face.

'You did what needed to be done,' she reassured, but her eyes were alight. 'Using the demon again doesn't mean you've relapsed.'

'Gives them something to think on at least, I can't imagine Cain will take this sitting down,' Kieran said as he tried not to look at the mess and focused on the woman in his care.

'And just where do you think you're going?'

They all looked up to see the maître d' skip down the stairs. Like a child with a secret, her arms deliberately hidden behind her back.

'I don't think that's any of your business really, is it?' Lorna grinned and dragged the tiny blonde off the stairs telekinetically, shoving her in Nick's direction as she tripped down the last couple of stairs.

'Nah, ah,' she called out as Kieran took to the stairs.

They turned to see her waving a small remote device as she fell back against Nick, giggling maniacally.

Kieran glanced up at Nick to see what he'd do.

'Run.' He glared at the pair of them.

'But?' Lorna paused.

'Just go. NOW.'

'No!' the blonde screamed as she pressed a button on the device. 'No survivors, NO SURVIVORS!'

Lorna picked Anna up in a fireman's lift and as the twins charged up the stairs with their cargo. Nick, having regained his angelic touch, used the grip he had on the female werewolf to kill her instantly, snatching up the device as she fell out of his hands.

Throwing it to one side he reached for the stairs, just as there was an explosion above him.

Kieran and Lorna dove out of the front door as the blast ripped the kitchens apart.

'Shit,' Aiden breathed as he helped catch them and they fell against the storefront opposite, sinking to the ground.

'Where's Nick?' Lorna searched the street. 'He should have been right behind us.'

'The blast might have knocked him out. I'll go check,' Aiden said as Kia and Ashlie ran over with the medics they'd called as soon as they'd heard shooting.

'Be careful!' Lorna yelled after him.

'I will.' He smiled and turned, stepping into the street.

Aiden scanned the restaurant for signs of movement through the glass but couldn't see any. As he reached for the door a larger explosion ripped through the basement causing much of the building above to creak and groan in threat of collapse.

The blast was enough to knock Aiden to the ground, his ears ringing.

By the time he'd regained his senses, the building was engulfed in flames.

Jumping up, he ran forwards, searching the street as he did so.

'NICK?! Nick, can you hear me?!' he yelled at the inferno, vaguely aware of sirens in the distance.

Finally registering Aiden's voice, Kia jumped up from where she was assisting the medic and ran over.

'Where is he?'

Aiden looked to Kia and back to the inferno.

'He's still in there.' Aiden scrubbed his hands over the stubble at his jawline, staring wide-eyed at the restaurant. 'My brother is still in there.'

Lorna was suddenly in front of both of them. 'We need to get away from here, the structure isn't sound.'

'You've got to be joking, if Nick's still in there I'm going in,' Kia took a step forward, but Lorna caught her arm, 'I can use a shield.'

'He might have used a fire exit in the basement when the kitchens blew,' Lorna reasoned, even as she stared into the ruins of the restaurant, willing Nick to appear. 'We don't know. But you can't go in there, the whole building is unstable,' she said, tugging them backwards as several fire engines arrived on the scene.

'I can't just stand here!' Kia yelled, trembling as tears welled in her eyes.

Kieran headed over as Lorna managed to drag Aiden away, her eyes wide as she gestured towards Kia.

'We could both go in?' Kieran offered, making his sister turn back on him with a glare.

'The hell you will,' she bit back.

'We're super-trained remember.' He shrugged in response.

With a sigh, Lorna ran her fingers through her hair and turned back to the restaurant as fire response teams set up their hoses.

'The fire crews have guardians for search and rescue, go and talk to them, tell them there may be someone still alive inside,' Lorna said gently. 'They might let you go with them with the right equipment, but I doubt it.'

'Everyone get back!'

Lorna glanced over her shoulder to see members of the fire crews running from the building.

While she held Aiden back, Kieran reached for Kia, throwing his arms around her, her screams hitting him in the chest as the building collapsed.

Fighting against his hold, she continued to scream until he had to give her a small electric shock to ground her.

'You have to let me go! I have to get to him, I can't lose him again, not like this!' Kia roared as she tried to walk through Kieran.

'What if he's not in there? What if he got out?' Kieran gripped her hard by the shoulders and gave her a little shake.

'What if he didn't?' Kia sobbed as she slumped to her knees.

TWO

As dawn broke, the full extent of the damage to Angelo's flagship restaurant and the building above it became clearer. A gaping hole, five storeys high, had opened up between the two neighbouring office blocks when the whole building had imploded in on itself.

Kieran walked up to where Kia stood, unmoving, her arms folded across her stomach, staring at the mass of rubble and smoke where the restaurant had been, a haunted look in her eyes, her face streaked with dried tears and soot.

'Kia?' He held a take-out cup of hot chocolate out towards her. 'Kia?' He repeated, louder the second time.

With a jolt of surprise, Kia took a deep breath and turned, taking the cup gratefully. 'Thank you.'

'They're not going to let us in there any time soon,' he soothed.

'Miss?' A member of the fire crew was suddenly stood in front of Kia holding out a spare uniform for her. He nodded reassuringly at them as Kieran took it for her while she tested the hot chocolate. 'With your help, we'll be able to get in there in the next couple of hours.'

When Kia simply nodded, the responder offered another nod of acknowledgement and left them.

'I've had a word with the supervisor,' Kia said, her voice monotone as she continued to stare straight ahead. 'They're going to let us go with them. You should get a uniform too.'

'There are a lot of bodies in there, do they know that?' Kieran asked, glancing over the wreckage again.

'Lorna has already told them what happened.' Kia shrugged, reaching forward and putting her cup down.

Kieran handed her the uniform, which included a pair of heavy-duty boots.

Smiling sadly, she unfolded the coveralls and, kicking her sneakers off, stepped into them, pulling them up over her jeans.

Aiden approached as she stepped into the boots and retrieved her hot chocolate.

'Dad just called, said he'll come down with Andrew if we need him.' Aiden paused, staring down at the cup of coffee in his own hands. 'I think he wants to be here, but I told him they're only letting you two in for now.'

'Yeah, let's just find him first,' Kia said as a heavily loaded pick-up truck pulled up and another search team began spilling out, already suited up and ready for briefing.

'I've sent Ashlie home, she looked dead on her feet,' Lorna said as she approached the group.

'Oh,' Kia looked up, distracted. 'Thanks.'

Kieran glanced over Lorna's shoulder to where Kia's friend Ashlie had been helping with Anna and Melody. He'd barely had a chance to speak to the bouncy blonde who had almost squeezed the life out of him for saving her best friend's life two nights before.

He'd not been in the mood to speak to anyone that night regardless. He wasn't sure it was worth making new friends in the pack if they were going to be as prone to funerals as some of those from his past. Since his parents and Jo had died, he'd kept to a very small bubble of people. It was generally just a bubble of one. Lorna.

Now Lorna came with a full pack of werewolves, something he was coming to terms with and learning to fight his own bias. That pack came with Kia and her work with the shelters, which also brought new people.

Scrubbing his hands over his face, he fought away the mental exhaustion.

Of course, throwing himself headlong into training as a Guardian HQ Medic to avoid dealing with his demons wasn't really helping on that front.

'Sir?'

Kieran opened his eyes to see one of the rescue team handing him another set of coveralls.

'Thank you,' he responded with a tired smile.

'Should you really be doing this?' Lorna was suddenly at his side, looking into his eyes with concern.

'I'll be fine,' he replied.

'That's not what I asked.' She reached out to pinch him but he dodged her, receiving a small zap of electricity for his trouble instead.

'We have a pack member to find.' He shot her a look. 'I'm not about to let Kia go in there by herself.'

Lorna glanced over at the almost catatonic Kia and nodded in agreement.

'Just be fucking careful,' she warned him.

With a fond smile, Kieran reached for the back of his twin's neck and pulled her in for a hug, kissing her hair before he let her go.

'I will,' he promised as he started pulling the coveralls on over his clothes.

'Give me your jacket,' Lorna instructed when he got the garment up to his waist.

Shrugging out of his dirty old leather jacket, the one he'd had since college, he slipped it around Lorna's shoulders. It drowned her, but he'd noticed the temperature was dropping. The grey morning clouds looked as though they were going to give way and dump a fresh covering of snow at any time.

And just because guardians and werewolves alike were less likely to feel the cold, that didn't mean he couldn't fuss over his sister when given the chance.

'If you don't find him . . . or if you do, and it's not good. Give her some air,' Lorna said with a nod in Kia's direction.

Kieran followed her line of sight and felt the twinge in his gut his sister knew he was feeling. He couldn't deny he felt an overwhelming need to keep Kia safe, even though he barely knew her. Even though she belonged to the angeling, heart and soul.

Even if he was stupid enough to have feelings for her, it could never come to anything.

'Don't be ridiculous. Don't go thinking like Nick was the other night,' he returned. 'Kia's just like a less annoying second sister.'

'Don't think I don't know how much of a lonely life you've led since that night.' Lorna raised both eyebrows at him.

'Single doesn't mean I have a death wish.' Kieran smirked as he zipped the coverall up. 'In fact, our head guardian over there was only giving me a pep talk about getting back out there just days ago.'

'She might have a point,' Lorna agreed.

'I might have enough on my plate right now.' Kieran rolled his eyes.

'Oh, speaking of which . . . it's almost New Year,' Lorna said suddenly coy.

'What's so special about New Year?'

'Aiden is taking the pack back in January and Acheron suggested it might be time to add some new pack members at the same time.' She winced playfully.

'What does that entail? Open house for hopeful wolves?'

'No, naming pack associates who aren't currently members as official members.' Lorna paused awkwardly. 'Kia's nominated Ashlie and Luca given Asha is already a member. I'd like to nominate you. If you're comfortable with the idea of course.'

Kieran was quiet long enough for Lorna to look worried.

He'd told Aiden to his face that he thought all werewolves were feral at the core and that he'd never trust them. He'd had to eat his words several times over since that night in October.

But family was important to Lorna, and the pack was the family she was fated to be a part of.

'I'm no longer *uncomfortable* with the idea,' Kieran admitted slowly. 'They're about to be my in-laws after all. If it means a lot to you as my family, well, just tell me what I have to do.'

Lorna smiled, relieved, and went to speak but he cut her off with a look of mock horror.

'I don't have to swear allegiance to your future husband or anything, right?!'

'No,' Lorna said through laughter. 'Nothing like that, it's more symbolic than anything else, it just means you're invited to meetings, kept in the loop, and though there would be a level of being there for the pack when it needs you, that kind of comes naturally anyway. It also works both ways.'

'Like tonight.'

'Like tonight,' Lorna agreed with a smile.

'Ready?' Kia was suddenly beside them. 'They're calling us for briefing.'

'Yep,' Kieran responded and looked to Lorna.

'Shield up at all times,' she instructed, unable to hide the concern in her eyes.

'I'm sure they'll tell us to do that anyway.' He nodded back.

'Aiden said something about doing a perimeter sweep of the surrounding blocks, in case he has come out of a fire exit somewhere.' Kia peered over her shoulder at Aiden.

'Good idea,' Lorna agreed and, shooting her brother another look, headed off to join Aiden who was speaking to one of the fire chiefs.

As Kieran steered Kia into the coffee shop down the street from Angelo's five hours later, Aiden and Lorna stood up to meet them.

'Any news?' Aiden asked immediately as Lorna gently manoeuvred Kia into a sofa before she could fall into it with exhaustion.

Kieran handed Kia a wet wipe from a pack one of the fire crew had given him as they'd been leaving the site. The coveralls and helmets they'd been wearing had saved them from most of the dust and dirt, but their faces bore soot from the residual fires they'd had to work around during their search.

'No sign of him,' Kia sighed and closed her eyes.

'How bad was it in there?' Lorna looked to Kieran, mentally asking him a different question.

'The collapse put some of the fire out, but the kitchen was still ablaze,' Kieran admitted. 'Though that did affect us getting as far as two of the original fire exits, we were able to relocate the bodies of the missing women, they're in a structural cavity that will take time to work around, but not everything was totally destroyed,' he said carefully.

'We didn't find anything either.' Aiden looked between them, barely covering the desperation in his own eyes. 'So now what?'

'The fires are finally all out, but it could be some days before specialist crews are able to work through that corner of the site due to the kitchen equipment,' Kieran explained.

'I haven't felt any harm come to him.' Kia peeled her eyes open. 'But I can't feel him either. Which could suggest he's unconscious.'

'Where else would he be?' Lorna frowned.

'Any one of the blocked exit tunnels.' Kieran shrugged. 'The positive news for now is that we haven't found his body, and Kia hasn't felt their link break.'

Finding the table full of pastries and sandwiches, Kieran grabbed a croissant and, tearing it in two, ate half in one go. He'd seen the state of Kia when her link with Nick had tried to tell her he was in a bad way. They all wanted to believe she was too calm for the worst to have happened.

'I'll grab you a coffee.' Lorna jumped up. 'We were starving and knew you two would be, so we grabbed a bunch of stuff. Kia, do you want tea?'

'Please,' Kia muttered and reached forward for a muffin to pick at.

'Lorna tells me she told you about the pack meet next week,' Aiden said, even though he was watching Kia carefully, Kieran knew the statement was for his benefit.

'Yeah,' Kieran returned around the second half of the croissant.

'She said you're OK with it.' Aiden dragged his eyes from Kia to his future brother-in-law cautiously.

Kieran had to fight the inner smirk.

Aiden would never be afraid of Kieran, he'd made that much clear over the months since they'd first met, well, clashed. But he didn't want to piss his intended's brother off any more than necessary either.

He let a slow smile spread across his lips as he looked to the werewolf.

'I'll go wherever my sister needs me to go,' Kieran said with a shrug before pausing long enough that Aiden seemed about to take it further. 'I'll do whatever it takes to be part of the family she has chosen.'

'Even if it means hanging out with furry mongrels?' Aiden offered a smirk of his own.

Shit. Yes, he had called them that at one point.

'So long as I get to shoot the next wolf who tries to bite her.' Kieran grinned.

'No wolves are allowed to bite her,' Kia mumbled, 'Too risky.'

'Given the circumstances, Lorna's blood would kill any wolf who tried to bite her, certainly none of our pack would be stupid enough to try it. So, in the circumstances that a wolf does attempt it, go right ahead.' Aiden waved the comment off. 'It's unlikely to be one of ours.'

'Who are you threatening to shoot now?' Lorna asked, reappearing with the drinks.

'Any wolf dumb enough to try and bite you,' Aiden admitted as she slid a black coffee in his direction.

Lorna scoffed.

'I'd like to see one try.'

'Not funny,' Kieran stated.

'Still too soon?' she goaded, before sticking her tongue between her teeth.

'Apparently so,' Aiden said lightly and reached for her hand as she sat back down.

'Speaking of biters, weren't you supposed to be at vamp HQ this morning?' Kieran looked to his sister.

'Yeah, but I used the circumstances to give my apologies,' Lorna explained, reaching for a hot chocolate with her free hand as Kia curled in on her cup of tea.

'What a pity,' Kia snarked, attempting to remain part of the conversation long enough to drink her tea.

'At least Declan tolerates me. It's some of his staff that can't wait to see the back of me.' Lorna shrugged.

'He's a smarmy bastard if you ask me.' Kia shrugged.

'Hillary is probably long-dead.' Kieran yawned and reached for a lemon muffin. 'How do they definitively know if a vampire has been dusted?'

'They don't. She has to be registered as missing for fifty to one hundred years. They can sleep that long if they choose to go to ground but rarely longer without food.'

'As next in line for the council seat, they can't possibly give her that long,' Kieran pointed out. 'It's been three months already and she was seen walking from the prison complex. Where the hell could she go?'

'She was seen?' Kia's eyes slid to Lorna.

'Declan had the prison swept, he says she was caught on camera.' Lorna nodded.

'Hmm.' Kia returned to her tea.

'Just because Casey was dead, doesn't mean she wasn't still a target,' Lorna pointed out, 'He had friends in dark places. But she might just have wanted out.'

'Back to it tomorrow then?' Kieran asked.

'No. Tomorrow we have a meeting with Mia, all of us, so I suggest we call it a day.' Lorna glanced at her phone for the time.

'I should stay here,' Kia mumbled.

'We were discharged for the day, but rescue crews will keep going, they know there's people in there, Nick especially. They told us they'd call if they found anything else.'

'I can't just go home when he could be pinned under rubble,' Kia bit back.

'You can't help him in this state,' Aiden said bluntly.

'How about we go back to the apartment? It's close by if anything gets called in and we need to be in the city in the morning anyway,' Kieran offered. 'Get a few hours' sleep.'

'We'll go back to the house and report back,' Aiden said as Kia reluctantly nodded.

THREE

Kieran let himself into Mia's office and found it empty. With a sigh, he fell down onto one of the sofas. It had been a long morning.

Kia had accidentally woken him when she'd left the apartment at 3a.m. though he had to admit that he'd been sleeping lightly in case she needed him, his hearing on super high alert. After a bath, she'd passed right out, and seemingly stayed that way until the early hours.

The meeting with Mia wasn't until eleven, so though he could guess where she'd gone, instead of following her, he'd headed for Guardian HQ to see if he was needed there.

He couldn't sleep any more, he'd also crashed out as soon as he'd managed a quick shower after making sure Kia had gone to bed. Even so, he'd had way more than the four-to-six hours he'd become accustomed to since working as a trainee medic.

He'd just closed his eyes to take in the peace when he heard voices from the corridor.

'Wow, look at the state of you!' Lorna appraised as she burst through the door with Mia and Kia in tow.

'Is any of that blood on my couch?' Mia asked with disgust.

Kieran tugged at a clean patch on his scrubs shirt, peering down at the mess.

'The body was in front of me, so I doubt it,' he groused.

'Rough morning?' Lorna's face dropped with concern.

'Something like that, D.O.A an hour ago, she was in an awful state.'

'Mia told me,' Lorna admitted causing her brother to scowl.

'Where've you been?' Kieran turned his attention on Kia as she sat beside him her arms full of brown paper bags. 'Actually, it doesn't matter if those bags are full,' he teased but his stomach rumbled at the smells wafting from within the paper.

'Breakfast.' Kia grinned brightly and handed him one of the bags.

'Mine?' he asked hopefully.

'All yours.' Kia nodded before handing Lorna and Mia a bag each.

Kieran tore into the packaging to find a large bacon and egg baguette. He groaned appreciatively but paused to take his shirt off before diving into the bag. The black vest he wore underneath wasn't spotless, but it smelled less of blood.

'Ben has some spare shirts in the cupboard if you want one?' Mia smiled as Kieran dropped the shirt on the floor.

'In a moment, too hungry,' he admitted before taking a large bite.

'There's coffee too,' Kia chuckled as Mia began sharing them around. 'How long have you been here?'

'I headed down not long after you snuck out.' Kieran shot her a look.

'Ah,' Kia looked sheepish. 'Sorry, I didn't mean to wake you.'

'I think I was ready to wake up, I was out cold as soon as I hit the pillow,' he said around his second mouthful. 'Did you find anything?'

'He's not there,' Kia announced.

'You're sure?' Lorna frowned.

'You weren't with her?' Kieran looked up over his food to where Mia and Lorna had taken seats and were extracting their own brunches from bags.

'Didn't even know she'd gone.' Lorna shot Kia an interested look. 'She called to offer to grab food an hour ago.'

'Almost certain.' Kia nodded and reclined on the sofa with her coffee.

'Where's your food?' Kieran narrowed his eyes at her.

'She's eaten it already,' Lorna said for Kia.

'I couldn't wait,' Kia said with a shrug.

Kieran swallowed his latest mouthful, staring at her for just a little too long. If she had an appetite, chances were she was telling the truth.

'If he's not at the site, where could he be?' Lorna asked. 'Aiden and Acheron were going to head down there when I left.'

'I already called Aiden.' Kia shook her head. 'Chances still are he's unconscious in one of the tunnels nearby, so he's going to search those with Acheron while we're here.'

'Alright then,' Lorna said slowly. 'And you,' she turned her attention on her brother, 'you're not planning on staying on for the night shift you had tonight, right?'

'I'll grab a nap in one of the bunk rooms later,' Kieran offered.

'I think you need a day off,' Mia said softly.

'I'll be fine.' Kieran waved them both off, wanting to finish eating his baguette in peace. 'Don't you now have two missing pack members?'

'Yes,' Lorna admitted. 'The rest of the pack is looking for Danyl.'

'Any chance Nick is wherever he is?' Mia glanced up from spearing a forkful of pancakes.

Lorna and Kia's eyes met quickly.

'Foul play?' Kieran interjected when they were all quiet for a touch too long.

'From an explosion?' Lorna rolled her eyes at her brother.

He shrugged and glanced at Kia, who he could tell was seriously considering it.

Kia met Kieran's eyes as Lorna went back to her own baguette.

'I take it we're waiting for Ben?' Kieran turned his attention on Mia.

'No, Ben is at a council meeting,' Mia said quickly before shovelling another mouthful of pancakes past her lips.

All three guardians looked at her at once.

'Aren't we supposed to know when those are taking place?' Kia's eyes darted between Mia and Lorna.

'Technically speaking.' Mia's eyes narrowed to show she was also less than impressed by the proceedings. 'He received the summons late last night.'

'It's as if they knew we'd all be detained this morning. Including you,' Lorna shot Mia a look, Mia was usually first point of contact for the HQ.

'What could be so urgent?' Kia deadpanned.

'I'm sure it's nothing to worry about.' Mia shrugged after a moment.

'When they don't inform us it's usually a status report,' Lorna informed Kia. 'However, with the circumstances as they are, they might be getting a little desperate over the vampire situation. That or Declan is pushing harder than I thought.'

It had never sat well with Kieran or Lorna that head guardians weren't invited to council meetings. Lorna especially hated being the patsy for all the deadliest executions in town. Back when witches had a spot on the council, it hadn't been the case, but since Lucious decided they were the perfect task force to keep the other creatures in check, they'd frequently been too busy or too dead to attend.

Since meeting the being himself, Kieran finally understood that his choice to entrust elemental witches with the role of guardians was actually borne out of immense respect for his kind. So much so, that the reason he didn't often train them was because he didn't consider they needed it.

'Don't emergency meetings get called by Lucious himself?' Kia asked quietly, something behind her eyes making her pale.

Kieran opened his mouth to ask her what she thought that meant, then realised that if anyone knew for definite whether something had happened to the angeling, Lucious would, and decided against it.

'With any luck, he's come down off his mountain to bestow the title of head vamp on Declan. Hillary could be filed as missing presumed dust so that everyone can move on and let me get back to something constructive here rather than spending time I don't have at the Vampiric Consulate trying to find clues as to where she fucked off to.'

'Anything I can help out with?' Kia waggled her eyebrows.

'To let you hack their systems I'd have to smuggle you in.' Lorna shook her head. 'As current head guardian, you should have more respect than I do in that building, but that doesn't seem to be the case, and not everyone is rolling out the red carpet for me as it is.'

'Charming,' Kia stated, heavy on the sarcasm.

'Holding me accountable is their way of punishing me in just about the only way they can. My diddled DNA means they can hold sway, otherwise they wouldn't want dogshit like me under their feet.'

'Aren't most of the day staff creatures on payroll or familiars?' Mia folded the remnants of her breakfast back into the bag before dropping it in the trash can behind her desk.

'Surprisingly not.' Lorna shook her head. 'About half are older bloodsuckers who don't sleep much in the day anymore and need something to do or have their noses in.'

'Interesting,' Mia said, raising her eyebrows.

'So why are we here?' Kieran asked through a yawn.

'Can't I just want to see you all?' Mia grinned.

'Not usually, no.' Lorna got up off the other sofa and started collecting everyone else's empty wrappers.

Kieran smirked. Mia and Ben, though they weren't blood related, were as close to grandparents as you could get in a city where no one aged at human speed. Though Kieran resented being told what to do in any capacity, and struggled with their authority, he could embrace the form of family they'd become. The couple had rescued the twins' mother from the U.S. and brought her up as their own in Pool Valley.

He'd been sniffing about the HQ stats since taking an active role within its walls. Mia and Ben had built the facility to better support city guardians and their adoptive daughter. Kieran had felt a sense of pride on discovering that the mortality rate of guardians within the Pool Valley boundaries had halved since the family set up home there.

The concept had proven so successful, they'd gone global. Which Kieran found delightfully underhanded, setting up supernatural businesses in the human-ruled world as a whole wasn't always easy, less so since the millennium witch hunts. He knew Mia would have been even more determined to find a way since having to run from her home.

'Are you setting up a new training scheme and need me here?' Lorna asked hopefully.

'Er, no. If I was, I'd need Kia.' Mia winced as Lorna's bright eyes switched to a glare. 'You're busy enough with the pack never mind the vamps.'

'I also have the pack, we could job share?' Kia offered.

'Not a bad idea,' Kieran said quickly before anyone could argue. 'When it's needed.'

'When it's needed,' Mia agreed. 'Then you can work something out between you.'

'Actually,' Kieran started but averted his eyes from his sister's, 'It will be needed. We now have two Lucious trained guardians in the building. There's a lot of knowledge share potential. I'm using some of it with the medics, we've already found ways to make medical advancements.'

'Good for you,' Lorna sniped.

'We'll still work on it together to see what differences there are,' Kia reassured. 'I don't know what everyone here is or isn't capable of. I'll need your help with that.'

'Knock it off, you're already stronger than most of us,' Kieran warned Lorna before she could telekinetically pinch either him or Kia.

'Pinch me, I'll hit back,' Kia warned with a grin.

The twins both rolled their eyes remembering Kia could hear them.

'All of you knock that off,' Mia ordered. 'I called you here because . . .'

Mia couldn't finish her explanation, because after a heavy-handed knock at the office door, Ashlie bumbled through it.

'Shit, sorry, am I late?' Ashlie stopped dead when she found three guardians staring at her.

'Because we have a new recruit,' Mia said with a smile, standing and offering Ashlie the seat next to Lorna.

Before she could awkwardly make it to the seat offered, Kia bounced up off her own perch and barrelled into Ashlie for a death-grip hug.

'What are you doing here? You insisted you'd never be registered!' Kia berated her friend, even as she retained her vice-like grip.

'Well, so did you once . . .' Ashlie shook her head mockingly, her curls bobbing around her shoulders. 'Sorry, do they know that?' She inclined her head awkwardly in the direction of Lorna and Mia.

'We know.' Lorna grinned.

'Thought I'd best come and lend your busy ass a hand,' Ashle continued with enthusiasm.

Kieran watched the embrace with interest. He'd barely caught a glimpse of Ashlie before Kia had smothered her, and on the occasions she had been around he'd been otherwise preoccupied. When Kia stepped back and started to re-introduce the clumsy blonde with jade-green eyes, he found himself acutely aware of the state he was in.

'Sorry, I'm fresh out of the medical unit, best you don't hug me,' he informed her before she'd had chance to speak.

'Oh. OK,' Ashlie stuttered.

'Smooth,' Lorna muttered under her breath as she got up to hug Ashlie herself, having briefly spoken with her the day before.

'Any news on Nick?' Ashlie asked quickly as she sat finally sat down.

'Well, he's not dead,' Kia answered. 'But we haven't found him yet either.'

'Could he be wandering about with concussion or something?' Ashlie asked, eyes wide.

'Something like that, we hope.' Lorna shot Kia a scowl.

'What, he could!' Kia said, a little too brightly for anyone's liking. 'I told you, I don't feel like he's dead.'

'Let's hope it stays that way.' Ashlie smoothed out her features, realising everyone else in the room was a little too serious in comparison to Kia.

'If I'd known you were coming, I'd have snagged extra food.' Kia rolled her eyes in Mia's direction.

'It's OK, I'm good.' Ashlie shrugged it off.

Though what she couldn't shrug off was the guardian sat next to her best friend. Kieran had barely taken his eyes off her since she'd entered the room. She had to assume he was sleep-deprived after the day before and the scrubs shirt at his feet. But if staring was the name of the game, she was more than happy to stare back at the man sitting across from her.

His dark shoulder-length hair was falling out of the low ponytail he'd clearly rushed and the black vest he seemed so awkward about gave her an excellent view of his arms. Strong, the guy works out, type arms.

'I've already talked Ashlie through the house rules and her registration,' Mia explained. 'Kia, Lorna, why don't you two show her around?'

'Kieran?' Lorna offered as she stood up.

'I should go get changed before I do anything else, I'll catch up.'

'Oh, before I forget,' Ashlie was saying to Kia as they prepared to leave, 'You, me, a giant pizza, soon.'

'Sure, when's your night off?'

'Shouldn't you be able to tell me that?' Ashlie whined playfully as they headed out the door.

As Kieran reached for the discarded scrubs shirt, he found himself hoping that pizza night would be at Kia's.

FOUR

Slipping a clean scrubs shirt over his head, Kieran let out a grunt when his phone began blaring in the locker he was about to leave it in for the night.

'Get changed and meet me at Broomstyx,' Lorna instructed when he answered the call.

'I'm about to start a shift, Lorna,' he ground out.

'Not tonight, you're not. We've found Danyl and need a medic, Mia will square it with your shift team.'

'Maybe I should keep my scrubs on?' Kieran mused aloud. He'd already packed the dirty vest into his kit bag and thrown his morning set of scrubs in the on-site laundry bin.

'That might be a good idea,' Lorna admitted.

Kieran noted the subdued tone in his sister's voice.

'That bad, huh?'

'Sounds it.'

Hanging up, he shoved his phone in the kit bag and slinging it over his shoulder, left the empty locker swinging open as he ran for the ground floor.

Ignoring Asha's concerned frown as he passed her in the bar, Kieran headed out onto the street where Lorna was in the Escalade with the engine running. Jumping in, he tossed his bag over his shoulder onto the back seat as Lorna pulled away.

'Where's Kia?'

'She's gone on ahead to see if there's anything she can do until you get there.'

'Where's there exactly?' Kieran asked, hastily buckling his seatbelt as Lorna sped across the city centre.

'You know I told you where I'd found Nick that night, beaten almost senseless . . .' Lorna trailed off as she glanced at her twin.

'Danyl's been found in the same place?' Kieran arched an eyebrow back at her.

'Yeah, exactly.'

The twins rushed to an Underground district which was part abandoned, part under renovation. There were ten identical subterranean apartment blocks on the gloomy street Lorna led her brother to. Kieran shuddered as he stared into the uniformity of the dark squares where windows had once been, carved into the rock of the city's underbelly. Those awaiting reno had had the windows smashed out, those under reno had windows covered with tarpaulin. He wasn't sure which looked more creepy.

Kieran wasn't surprised when Lorna took him to the front door of a block barely lit by emergency lighting with smashed windows. Last on the list, he assumed.

Seth was at the entrance, a haunted look on his face.

'They're on the second floor,' he said, his voice hollow.

'Is he . . .?' Lorna started but Seth shook his head.

'Not quite, but it doesn't look like it will be long. I'm not even sure he can be moved.' Seth handed her a black bundle. 'I think Acheron's hoping you guys can try though.'

Kieran looked down at the body bag and gave Seth a sombre nod as Lorna lay a hand on his shoulder before heading inside.

The smell hit them as soon as they entered the stale air of the apartment block.

'What is that?' Lorna said quietly as she baulked.

'It's hard to explain,' Seth said from the doorway, standing on the threshold as though he couldn't re-enter.

As they climbed the stairs to the second floor, the stench intensified, reaching its peak when they followed a trail of torch lights into an apartment without a front door. Well, it had a door, but it lay splintered on the floor where one of the pack had kicked it in.

The dwelling was gutted, stripped bare of any fixtures and fittings. Even the vinyl flooring was gone from the kitchenette. Danyl was laid out in the middle of the open plan living space, his brother Dante knelt beside him as Acheron and Aiden kept back, leaning against a nearby wall in silence, watching the exchange between the brothers.

It was instantly obvious to Kieran why Danyl couldn't be moved, and that there was very little he'd be able to do for the werewolf.

Kia, stood hunched in the darkest corner, her arms folded, barely looked up when they entered.

'Do we know what happened here?' Kieran asked gently.

'It looks as though they've been giving him some kind of acid bath, probably as a form of torture,' Aiden said quietly. 'We can't know the concentration, or quantity. It doesn't look like it's been happening here, but we did find him in the tub. As you can see, he doesn't have much skin left and the pain we caused him getting him this far was immense.'

Following his line of sight as Aiden glanced in the direction of the bathroom, Kieran pressed his lips tightly together to prevent his true feelings crossing his face. There were pieces of Danyl marking the journey where his burned and rotting flesh had started to fall from his bones.

Lorna's eyes were waiting when he drew his gaze back, he went to speak, but Lorna shook her head very slightly before turning to Aiden questioningly.

'Because we don't have a quick or painless way to do it,' Aiden muttered, making Dante flinch as he hunched over his felled brother, who was less than half the size he had been, a wasted mass at his knees. 'Not without a silver bullet or . . .'

'Nick,' Kia said flatly from where she was, staring in the direction of Danyl's empty eye sockets.

Although he could no longer see or speak, Danyl gave a confused grunt at the sound of her voice.

'You may see him soon, brother,' Dante mumbled.

Danyl let out a moan at the news, followed by a cry of anguish.

'Can you guys do anything? Anything at all?' Dante implored each guardian in turn.

'Nick's ability to end life peacefully never spread to me,' Kia admitted, 'I can't replicate that. The demon wings and the loss of morals is as far as I've ever got,' she said sadly, though she fought back a smirk. 'I've never been able to replicate the light orbs, angel wings, or his death-touch.'

'Ironic, considering he kept the demon away from you where possible until it was too late,' Dante scoffed.

'It's a DNA security thing.' Kia shrugged. 'If I could replicate it, any morph could.'

'I have a gun in the car, but it's not currently loaded with silver,' Lorna offered, reverting the conversation.

'That will have to do,' Dante said with a sigh. 'It will knock him out long enough to get him back to the house. I can't bear to see him in this much pain.'

Danyl's own silence on the matter suggested he agreed.

'OK,' Kieran started after a moment's awkward silence. 'Let's get him home.'

'Between the three of us, we should be able to get him to the car with minimal jostling.' Lorna nodded in agreement.

'You two lift and slide the body bag beneath him,' Kieran instructed as Lorna shook out the bundle she was still holding. 'I'll work on keeping him together as painlessly as possible.'

'You can do that?' Dante and Acheron said together.

'I'm going to try,' Kieran promised.

Once Kieran's telekinetic energy could be seen dancing over Danyl's body, Lorna and Kia used theirs to lift him towards the body bag.

The werewolves watched with bated breath, but there weren't any sounds of discomfort from their pack brother as the procedure took place.

Lorna watched the concentration on her brother's face as they began to transport Danyl out of the building.

'OK, *now I see why you wanted to do this,*' she transmitted.

'*Shh, you can apologise later,*' Kieran returned without taking his eyes from his patient.

By the time they loaded him into the escalade, Kieran had managed to send Danyl into a lucid state of unconsciousness.

The werewolves, leaving the guardians to their cargo, kept watch for anyone lying in wait. They all knew whoever attacked Danyl could be lurking.

'Kia and I have got this if you need to set the seats in your car.' Kieran glanced at his sister, wondering how the others were going to get back to the pack house before he spotted Aiden's car up the street.

They loaded Danyl into the back as gently as possible, Kieran managing to keep him stable as Dante climbed into the back to be with him and Kia jumped in the front ready for unloading at the other end.

'I'll stay with him, to keep him under as long as I can.' Kieran squeezed himself onto the rear loading bay as Lorna went to close the door.

'OK. Thank you.' She offered him a smile as she shut him in.

Expecting the guttural breathing from within the body bag to stop at any time, no one spoke as Lorna steered the Escalade through the city streets, Aiden's car right behind them.

'He hasn't got long,' Kieran said quietly as they hit the suburbs, rounding the mountains that would take them to MaryVaille.

'At least we didn't need to shoot him,' Dante said sadly, his fingers toying with the edges of the bag containing his brother.

As if on cue, Danyl drew his last breath as soon as the vehicle rolled onto pack grounds.

'He's gone,' Kieran announced for Dante, who swallowed hard and lay his hand on his brother's leg once he knew it wouldn't hurt him.

'Thank you,' Dante whispered as the car parked by the front door and he slipped past Kieran, who stepped back, out of the way, to let him carry his brother into the house for the rest of the pack to say goodbye.

'One found, one still to go,' Kia said on a sigh as she rounded the rear corner of the escalade to stand with him.

Hands on his hips, Kieran peered down at her, trying to gauge her mood.

'Do you think . . . ?'

'He'd have needed to be in a pretty poor state already. If they're . . .' Kia stopped when she had to fight a visible gag and shook her head. 'If they were doing that to Nick, I'd know about it.'

Kieran wanted to ask her if she was sure, but couldn't bring himself to venture down that avenue.

'Come on.' He slung an arm around her shoulders. 'Let's head inside with the others.'

Nodding, Kia let him guide her into the house and into the dining room where most of the pack were gathered, the mood solemn.

Clocking his sister, stood in solidarity with Aiden and Acheron, Kieran nudged Kia towards the kitchen. Scott, stood near the back, was the only one to speak, a gentle 'Hey, Kia,' with a squeeze of her shoulder as they stopped next to him.

Offering an exhausted smile and a nod, Kia was quickly distracted by Sookie sidling up next to her with mugs of something hot in her hands.

'Hey you two,' Sookie said with a smile, handing Kieran and Kia a mug of syrupy hot chocolate each, a stick of chocolate sticking up out of the foam.

'Thanks, Sookie,' Kieran said quietly as Kia let out a quiet noise of delight before eating her chocolate stick in two gooey bites.

'Well, at least you're eating.' Sookie eye-balled Kia as she stepped back.

Kieran watched Kia blush at the attention, and realised that Sookie had clearly gifted her youngest son that look. The one that told his beloved when she was being reckless.

Knowing it was none of his business, Kieran distracted himself by glancing out at the gardens in the darkness, noting the shovels leant against the terrace wall ready to mark Danyl's final resting place.

Swallowing down the defeatist sigh he'd caught himself preparing, Kieran couldn't help wondering where on earth the angeling was, and whether they'd find him in time.

Once words had been said and everyone had uttered their goodbyes silently or aloud, the wolves began to move their brother out onto the terrace.

'I can't quite believe it.' Lorna suddenly appeared next to Kia, dunking her own chocolate stick into another hot chocolate.

'It never gets any easier,' Kia muttered before sipping her own drink.

'Hasn't it crossed your mind what it must have taken to catch one of our strongest members in the first place?' Lorna shot Kia a look, ignoring the glare her brother fired her way. 'I'd been in that apartment before.'

'When you found Nick beaten up and half dead,' Kia stated. 'I'd been there before too. We found what we thought was the root of the trafficking gang down there.'

'And given Cain's brutes were working for the trafficking ring . . .' Kieran said to make sure he was on the right track.

'Exactly,' Lorna agreed. 'Though the traffickers had no reason to go after a random pack member when the aim of the trafficking network was to get to Nick and Kia directly.'

'But if they knew they were losing the chance to take Nick out, they might have been hoping to use Danyl as bait . . . until Nick got himself blown up and they didn't need Danyl anymore?' Kia said for Lorna with an arched eyebrow.

Sitting on the terrace wall with Kia as Danyl's grave was filled in some time later, Kieran watched as Kia became more and more closed off. Since the revelation his sister had forced her into, she'd clearly been dwelling on the matter harder than before.

With the discovery that Danyl had been murdered, there were weary eyes all around them, some stealing the odd glance in Kia's direction. She met each of them with a stoic nod.

'Do you want to leave?' Kieran muttered under his breath as he shifted his position on the wall, bringing his head momentarily closer to Kia's.

'Nick is alive until proven otherwise,' she returned, her yaw tight. 'I'll continue to search the vicinity of Angelo's for traces of his energy, until we hear further.'

'Do you want to head back down there tonight? The crew might have cleared some more,' Kieran offered.

'I need to be here tonight. It's only right,' she said after a moment's thought, but her voice was tight.

'And what if time is of the essence?' Kieran scowled.

'I can't think like that.' Her voice was hollow as she stared at the events unfolding beneath the terrace in the cemetery clearing.

'Are you two coming inside?' Sookie was suddenly stood behind them. 'There's more hot chocolate.'

'Is everyone staying for the wake?' Kia peered over her shoulder.

'Not everyone,' Sookie admitted. 'Aiden is insisting on ordering in shortly though for those who are staying.'

'Do you think they'd miss me for an hour?' Kia looked hopeful as she stood from the wall and let Sookie lead her towards the dining room.

'Why?'

'I need a moment in the office.'

'Sure.' Sookie smiled and they disappeared into the house, headed for the kitchen.

Kieran swiped back a stray lock of hair and stayed where he was. Lorna was walking towards him.

'They went to the kitchen,' he explained when she looked pointedly at the spot Kia had occupied.

'Does she want to get back to it?'

'Not yet.' Kieran shook his head and stood to join his sister. 'How is everyone taking it?'

'Shock mostly, I don't think the implications have quite sunk in yet. Let's not speculate any further either.' Lorna folded her arms and glanced over her shoulder at the wolves making their way back on to the terrace. 'Aiden is on the same page, Acheron most likely too.'

'Do you think the New Years meet will go ahead?'

'I think Aiden might use it to draw Cain out.' Lorna met her brother's eyes.

'What am I getting myself in for?' Kieran asked with a smirk.

'Nothing you don't want to,' Lorna admitted earnestly.

'You're kidding, right?' Kieran scowled down at her.

'I know how you feel about werewolves . . .'

'How I felt about werewolves,' Kieran reminded her. 'If this friendly bunch of fluffballs is about to be attacked by a rabid bunch of mangeballs, I won't stand aside and let you, or Aiden, handle that alone.'

'They're not that friendly when it comes down to it.' Lorna punched him lightly on the arm.

'As I've witnessed,' Kieran agreed. 'But if something has happened to Nick at their hands, you'll need all the help you can get, you said so yourself.'

'Alright,' Lorna said softly a smile lighting her eyes.

'Your family, my family.' Kieran grinned before dragging her into his arms.

'It's not like you have a choice, when I'm all that's left.' Lorna smirked.

'Don't let Mia hear you say that.' Kieran offered her a look of shock.

'By blood, then, at least.'

Kieran nodded as the last of the mourners edged their way back into the house to the dining room.

FIVE

As Kieran sat back in his seat at the dining table, chewing the last mouthful of beef noodles from the giant spread of Asian fusion food decorating the surface in front of him, a commotion broke out in the hall.

Jumping up without thinking, he went to where Aiden and Acheron were trying to talk sense into Kia, who was hysterical by the time Kieran joined in.

'Kia, what's happened?' Kieran asked gently as Lorna stepped up behind him.

'I don't know, I just . . .' she shook her hands violently as she spoke. 'I feel . . .'

They all watched as she turned in a full circle and stared at the ceiling like she was trying to stop the tears long enough to concentrate.

'Take a moment,' Kieran offered as Aiden and Acheron took a step back to give her some air.

'We went into the office to see how she was after food and she was sitting in a trance.' Acheron explained as Kia tried to get a grip.

'When I reached out to collect her empty plate, she jumped up like this.' Aiden finished for his father, though the haunted look in his eyes as he still held the crockery in his hands gave Kieran the shivers.

'Pain,' Kia gasped. 'Lot's of pain.'

'Do you need to sit down?' Lorna gestured back towards the office.

'Not mine. His.'

They all felt silent as she bent double like she could throw up.

'I need to go.' Kia righted herself, swiping her bedraggled black curls back off her face.

'Where?' Acheron asked and looked to the hall as if to march for his coat.

'I just need to go.' She shook her hands again and edged towards the hall herself.

'Is he . . .?' Aiden started, but Acheron shook his head.

'No.' Kia snapped. 'But I need to go.'

Kieran looked at Lorna, who was looking at Aiden.

'I'll go with her.' Kieran offered, knowing they had a wake in progress already.

'OK.' Aiden agreed with a relieved sigh. 'But call us as soon as you need us.'

'Sure thing.' Kieran nodded as Kia rushed around him and Lorna palmed him her car keys with a returned nod.

Rushing out to the car after Kia, Kieran unlocked the car before she could reach it so she knew which one to jump in as he caught up with her.

'Where to?' he asked as he started the engine.

'Central.'

'Near Angelos?'

'I think so.' Kia fidgeted in her seat as he threw the car down the drive and on to the main road as fast as the road would allow.

Kia hard locked her focus on her window but continued to fidget as Kieran sped into the city. He stole several glances her way but could tell something was different about her panic. Nick wasn't dead. Or at least not yet.

As they drew closer to the city centre Kia went back into a trance.

Kieran considered stopping the car, but soon realised she was concentrating.

'Next left.'

'OK.' he replied gently.

'Right here.'

Kieran manoeuvred through the city streets at each of her commands, even running a couple of red lights when she yelled at him to do so.

With her eyes closed she was working on pure feeling, but Kieran could tell they'd done a wonky loop through the city streets and avenues.

'Is he on the move?' Kieran finally asked pulling over.

'What makes you ask that?!' Kia's eyes snapped open but quickly squinted as she tried to work out where they were.

'We've been down this avenue three times now,' Kieran said gently.

'He must be.' Kia leaned forward in her seat and looked up and down the road. Eventually she turned in her seat. 'Back that way.'

'Is he underground?'

'I don't think so.' Kia rubbed her forehead and took a moment. 'Have you noticed any vans or trucks on the same streets?'

'Someone moving him?'

'I don't know. I thought we were getting close. He feels so close.'

Her breathing hitched as though a panic attack might set in before she let out a scream and punched the dashboard.

'FUCK.'

Kia put her head in her hands and elbows on the dash as she stared down the street.

'I've lost him,' she mumbled after a deep breath. 'I can't feel him anymore.'

'Shit,' Kieran spat. 'Do you want to go underground, see if you pick him back up.'

'If I could feel him from MaryVaille, I'd know if he was underground,' Kia groused. 'Thank you for not assuming the worst just then.'

'Kia, I've seen the worst, remember.'

She offered him a silent nod and opening the door to the Escalade, slipped out onto the sidewalk.

Kieran watched her pace a few feet, one hand on her hip, the other tangled in her hair as she tried to work out what to do. She stopped and stared up the street again. Kieran did another perimeter check before getting out of the car and joining her, placing his hands on her shoulders.

'Just tell me where you want to go next?'

'Can we just sit in the car and see if I get the feeling back?' Kia asked after a minute.

'Sure,' Kieran whispered and went back to the driver's seat.

Kia circled the car, looking up and down the street several times. Kieran watched her in the headlights, hands on her hips, lost look in her eyes and no regard for the tumbling temperatures as the clock crept towards midnight and the threat of snow lingered in the streetlights.

'How far are we from Angelo's?' Kia asked as she climbed back into the passenger seat.

'Couple of blocks that way.' Kieran jerked his thumb over his shoulder. 'He could be disorientated in a tunnel somewhere?'

'No, Aiden, then I, searched all the tunnels.' Kia's eyes continued to search the street as though she was searching for an answer.

'What if there's a blocked one?'

'I'd need city planning papers for that.' Kia admitted. 'There was nothing obvious blocked, unless it ran under the site and the bomb opened something up.'

'It's possible,' Kieran encouraged.

'It is.' Kia mumbled.

'Let's sit here another twenty minutes or so, then I think you need some sleep–'

'I'm fine.'

'Kia, I'm not saying give up. I meant we'll go back to the apartment, at least then if he pops back up on your radar we're not too far away. You can also tell the site crews what you felt once they're back at it in the morning.'

With a sigh of resignation, Kia sat back in her seat and closed her eyes for a while.

'Alright. You make a lot of sense.'

'At least you felt something.'

'That's true.' Kia rubbed her own arms as if the fact in itself was comforting.

Kieran eased back in his seat and eyed the clock, but within ten minutes Kia was asleep in the passenger seat.

SIX

Fighting a yawn, Kieran cut the engine and glanced down at his scrubs shirt, hoping it wasn't too dirty. He hadn't had time to change. Lorna had promised him the New Years meeting wasn't until mid January, but Aiden had called it a few days early in light of the loss of Danyl and the fact Nick was still missing.

It had been too late to move his shifts around and so he'd pulled a double, covering for Lana who would cover for him for the next two days.

The drive was awash with cars, he was glad he'd taken his motorbike.

Dropping his rucksack from his shoulders into one hand, he made his way towards the house.

As he wove through the crowd of vehicles, the driver's door of a blue compact opened with sudden force, narrowly missing him.

'Oh shit, I'm sorry, almost got you there!' a bright voice met him from the driver's seat.

'Only almost,' Kieran said with a smile as Ashlie swung her bag out onto the gravel before her heeled feet. 'Here, let me get that for you.'

Kieran reached down for her bag to give her more space to get out of the car.

'Thank you,' she returned the smile as she got out of the car and shut the door. 'Oh hey, you're Kia's roommate.'

'Ashlie, right?' Kieran asked with a nod.

'That's me,' she agreed and held her hand out for her bag.

'I think I can manage up to the house,' Kieran offered and nodded her onwards.

'I'm not going to stop you.' Ashlie grinned and began leading the way.

They walked a couple of awkward steps before Ashlie spoke again.

'We're not late, are we? Kia couldn't get me covered at the shelter, I had to wait for the evening relief.'

'I don't think they can start without everyone here, and I was also detained.' Kieran tugged at his shirt in demonstration.

'You're going to want to change that,' Ashlie said as she glanced back over her shoulder. 'What is that? Vomit?'

'Ugh, probably.' Kieran looked down at the stain he hadn't spotted. 'I thought the patient missed. Apparently not.'

'Hazzard of the species, am I right?' Ashlie offered him a knowing smile as they were bathed in the light of the open front door.

'Hey, you guys, thanks for coming at shorter notice.' Aiden was at the door as they crossed the threshold.

'Sorry we're late,' Ashlie spoke for them both, making Aiden raise an amused eyebrow at Kieran.

'That's OK, you're not the last, Kia's not back yet.' Aiden's amusement turned to concern as both Kieran and Ashlie almost caused themselves whiplash looking at him.

'Do you want me to go back for her?' Kieran put Ashlie's bag down at her feet and turned back to the door.

'No, hopefully that won't be necessary, she answered her phone twenty minutes ago and promised she was on her way.' Aiden sighed, then ran his fingers through his hair as he looked from Kieran to Ashlie and back again. 'But maybe stand by. You'll have time to change at least.'

Nodding, the guardians left Aiden in the hall and began heading to their designated rooms for the night. Kieran finding Lorna had allocated him the room opposite hers on what was becoming a permanent basis.

'How's she been?' Ashlie asked quietly as they headed up the stairs.

'Kia?' Kieran looked back to Aiden, who was leaning against the door frame and watching the driveway. 'Well, when she's not searching for Nick, she's sleeping off the exhaustion that follows.'

'I haven't heard from her, but I didn't want to pry without news, I've offered to help around my shifts, but she didn't answer me.'

'The first couple of days she tried to balance searching with dismantling Jamie's computer system and her mother's empire in the hopes she'd find something that might give her a better clue on where to look if he was snatched.'

'She's getting desperate,' Ashlie stated when they reached the top of the stairs.

'Can you blame her?'

'I've never let anyone get close enough to know how that feels,' she muttered.

'Well, it sucks,' Kieran affirmed.

'Sorry.' Ashlie grimaced, her pale green eyes wide.

'Don't be, it was a long time ago. I'm down here.' Kieran tossed his head in the direction of the east wing.

'I'm this way.' Ashlie backed up a step in the opposite direction.

'See you at dinner.' Kieran offered another smile as she turned away.

He fought the urge to glance down the hall to see which room Ashlie was in as he entered his bedroom. With a heavy sigh, he dropped his rucksack on the bed and shrugged out of his jacket before peeling off the filthy scrubs shirt.

He'd barely seen Kia since the night of Danyl's wake. After he'd taken her back to the apartment and steered her zombie-style into her room, she'd left before he got up the next day.

Lorna and Aiden were on high alert, even having to go down to the bomb site to collect her after a rescue worker had found her asleep in the back of his truck, hoping no one would notice if she took a quick snooze rather than going home.

'Thought I sensed you.'

Kieran looked up to see his sister walk in the room as he reached for a clean t-shirt from his bag.

'You sensed right.' He smiled as he pulled the elastic from his hair and shook it out. 'Kia back yet?'

'She just walked in.' Lorna gestured towards the hallway.

'How did she look?'

'Shattered.' Lorna met his eyes. 'Dead on her feet.'

Kieran knew the look well, Kia must have looked like hell.

His sister's warning couldn't have prepared him for just how awful Kia looked. When he found her in the kitchen ten minutes later, she looked hollow, devoid of emotion, haunted.

'On the booze already?' Kieran offered a soft smile as he leant on the counter next to her.

Kia slammed the two shot glasses she'd drained down and glared at him.

'It's espresso.'

'Can I get one of those?' Kieran asked as she began reloading the coffee machine.

'Sure,' she snarled.

'Can I help?'

She shrugged and handed him a refilled glass.

'A fresh pair of eyes might help.'

Without looking up, Kia nodded reluctantly before turning on her heel and heading for the dining room.

'We're waiting for you.' Lorna's head appeared around the doorframe Kia had gone through.

'Sorry,' Kieran flustered as he straightened and joined his twin.

The last of the stragglers were in the process of taking a seat as they entered the dining room. Kia found the seat Ashlie had been saving for her, Kieran sat with Lorna.

'Now that we're all here, let's begin,' Aiden said as he reached for a bread roll from a selection of both hot and cold food displayed down the middle of the table. 'Acheron?'

'As you are all aware, we're gathered here tonight to reinstate Aiden as pack alpha and welcome some new associates. In the light of recent events, this is lower key than is standard, but necessary all the same. Are there any opposed to Aiden's return as Alpha?'

Kieran found his eyes scanning the pack members across the table from him for any signs of discomfort, and given the recent events, was surprised not to find even the slightest hint of uncertainty.

'Motion passed. Aiden.' Acheron offered a nod to his son.

'Thank you.' Aiden offered a nod to the room. 'We also have two new member proposals . . .'

'Four.'

Everyone looked to the voice from the hallway as the front door closed behind whoever had let themselves in.

At the sound of the voice many wolves had flinched, preparing to stand, but Aiden had held a hand up for pause.

Before Kieran's confusion had time to catch up, two werewolves appeared in the doorway. Acheron moved in front of Sookie and Kia glanced at Aiden with questioning eyes.

'I'm not here to fight,' the first werewolf said, his eyes flitting from Aiden to Kia and back.

'Then what do you want, Cain?' Aiden asked calmly.

'I thought I just made that obvious. I want back in.'

'Never going to happen,' Aiden replied. 'You think a single member of this pack would vote you back in after what you did?'

'What did I do?' The look of innocence on the man's face wasn't fooling anyone.

'You know what you did, you murdering bastard,' Kia hissed between gritted teeth.

'Now, now, Aiden, I'd muzzle that one if I were you. Speaking for the alpha. Tut tut. Your dead brother's ex has less claim to a space in this pack than I do after all.'

'There is no proof that my brother is dead.'

'Other than the insanity of his partner.' Cain grinned at Kia. 'Murderess that she is.'

'Whatever allegations you hold against Kia, I would advise you tread carefully,' Aiden warned. 'She is head guardian and any death at her hands you wish to make light of may not be pack business. I'm not so sure you'll find the results you seek by taking your complaint to the council either.'

Cain's right-hand man glanced at Kia as Cain recomposed himself, staring evenly at Aiden, Kia grinned back. Kieran fought a smirk, knowing that Cain had just implicated himself as part of the Evelyn incident. Kia hadn't had reason to kill any other wolves recently, other than those working for her mother, Kia was ahead of the mutt.

'Forgive my rudeness, this is my second, Sean.' Cain finally acknowledged the wolf with him. 'Let's get back to business. We want in.'

'Barnes pack, I table the motion to reinstate ex-member Cain and welcome his associate, Sean. Any takers?' Aiden deadpanned as he stared Cain down.

The rest of the pack, also focused on Cain, remained silent.

'You have your answer,' Aiden stated.

Between them, Kieran knew Lorna was wound tight like a spring, ready to go for the jugular and prepared for an ambush. Sliding his eyes sideways, he let her know he wasn't sensing that kind of threat and her nails retracted slightly from the table-top.

'Well, of course I had hoped it wouldn't come to this.' Cain sighed dramatically. 'I intend to bring this murdering, mongrel pack back in line. I've seen the atrocities you let your brother and his bitch do in the name of this pack and it's a disgrace to the species to let non-wolf members act that way. If you won't let me in, I'll have to take it from you.'

Several pack members growled and shifted in their seats, including Lorna, Kieran caught Aiden place a hand on her knee under the table before he stood up.

'Then I suggest you go away and draft up a proposition for me and we'll review the suggestions with Saracen O'Niell present.'

'You can't hide behind another pack.'

'I don't intend to. It's protocol if you wish to challenge for ownership of another pack. Not that you are registered to one, legally. We are aware of your current standing as leader of an unofficial pack.'

It was Aiden's turn to grin when Cain realised Aiden had prepared for such a gauntlet.

'Nothing about him is legal,' Scott scoffed.

'You can't prove anything.' Cain glared at the second outburst.

Aiden again held a hand up for calm.

'Until you have made an official challenge, I suggest you tell your wolves to keep away from all Barnes pack members until the challenge is on the table, or the next time a guardian comes knocking at your door, it might not be in self-defence.'

'Is that a threat?'

'It's a promise,' Lorna stated.

'I trust you will instruct your members in the same manner, especially that.' Cain nodded to Kia.

'Kia is partly out of my control, but keep to your side of the bargain and she'll have less reason to bother you,' Aiden said with a smile. 'Now I suggest you escort yourselves off Barnes property before I let her chase you off it.'

Cain shot another look at Kia, who stood.

'I hope your *new recruits* know what they're getting themselves in for.' Cain gave Ashlie, then Kieran, a pointed look.

Kieran felt his body temperature rise at the thought of the bastard harming anyone in the room, but his eyes were torn to Ashlie who had more of a choice to be there than he did.

'Cain, how did you know this meeting was tonight?' Acheron asked, clearly suspicious.

'Let's just say an angel came to me.' Cain laughed, especially when Ashlie placed her hand on Kia's stomach as she involuntarily nudged forwards. 'See you round.'

Following them to the door, Aiden watched until their car was back on the open road.

'You want him to challenge you?' Kia was stood behind him with her arms folded and eyes narrowed when he finally closed the door and turned. Lorna was with her.

'What the hell are you thinking?' Lorna hissed.

'I want to know where I stand. Where we all stand.' Aiden looked to them both in turn but held Lorna's gaze. 'It's better that he drags this shit out into the open than continues to strike by stealth.'

'Do you think he has Nick?' Kia whispered.

'I think he was baiting you.' Aiden gave her a pointed look. 'Let's get back to business.'

'I think he at least knows as much as we do about what happened to Nick,' Kieran muttered as she passed where he stood leaning against the dining room doorframe. 'Need me to cover you?'

'We'll talk later,' Kia uttered under her breath without looking at him and returned to her seat.

SEVEN

Giving Lorna's shoulder a squeeze to suggest she go to bed, Kieran finally decided it was bed time. He couldn't listen to the debate about what Cain would try next any longer. The wolves had been going round in circles about it since dinner.

The twins had offered their opinions and non-wolf viewpoints, but it was reaching stalemate over whether Aiden should accept any challenge Cain would lay down.

The look on his sister's face told him Aiden would accept it out of etiquette more than anything, and that the argument was pointless.

Having watched Ashlie and Kia leave the room together, he'd assumed Kia was OK, until he'd seen Ashlie head towards the stairs by herself.

'We could have done with Asha here,' Lorna mumbled suddenly.

'Why isn't she?' Kieran turned back briefly.

'Like you, struggled to get her shifts covered. They were understaffed too, and Luca is with her. They gave their consent to both motions ahead of the meeting.' Lorna shrugged. 'It's not unusual, just shitty timing.'

'Let's hope he gives us enough notice next time.'

'With Saracen needing to review the challenge, whatever it might be, you'd hope so. He's a busy wolf himself.' Lorna fought a yawn.

'Go to bed, it might be the distraction he needs if you do.' Kieran inclined his head in Aiden's direction. 'I'm going to check on Kia then head up myself.'

'You might have a point,' Lorna said with a tired smile and tipped her head onto his shoulder.

Kissing the top of his sister's head, Kieran paused for a moment before leaving them to it.

He found Kia in the small office next to Sookie's den. It too was wall-to-wall books.

'Hey, are you alright?' Kieran wandered in and stood beside her, his arms folded.

'I will be, when I get that prick.' Kia was staring intently at the screen.

'What are you up to?'

'I've been going through my mother's accounts and files to work out exactly what the business arrangement was that she had with Cain. There has to be one on here somewhere. So far all I've got is loose threads and payments.'

With a sigh, Kia leant back in the chair, having realised she'd been sat with her nose practically against the screen.

'How bad is it?' Kieran grabbed the vacant chair next to her, assuming it was the one Ashlie had been using and helped himself to a seat.

'She's worked with a LOT of werewolves over the last five years. I've been making a list so I can dig into the background and location of every single one. Cain's name doesn't come up directly, but I suspect Sean's will.' She glanced at him, rubbing her eyes, 'That or there'll be an obvious alias in there when someone on the list is short a background check.'

'She knew you could do all that, so did Jamie.'

'But Cain might not.' Kia pointed at him.

Kieran watched her for a moment, concerned by the hardened exterior she was trying to present through extreme fatigue.

'Surely Aiden knows where Cain is holed up?'

'Probably. He'd also need an address to form a pack.'

'You think he'll do that? Go legit if he over-threw Aiden.'

'He doesn't want this pack in anything but name. He's got his own wolves, we know that. There are also too many wolves on this list for them all to be lone. But I'll check that against the registry when I'm next in HQ, I get better access from there.' Kia shrugged. 'Has everyone else gone to bed?'

'Not quite.' Kieran offered her a smirk. 'Aiden is being grilled by stragglers about what he'll actually do. I left Lorna nodding off at his side.'

'There's nothing he can do right away. He needs to see the terms of the challenge.'

'Yes, they've been over that, at least fifty times so far.' Kieran resisted the urge to rub his own eyes in frustration, it had been a tedious evening, and his shift-addled brain wasn't really up for it. 'If Cain isn't legal, surely he doesn't have a footing?'

'If he chooses to play dirty there are all sorts of footings he could use.' Kia raised both eyebrows pointedly.

'The wolves you killed as part of your mother's operation were beyond pack business, surely?'

'You'd like to think so, but I think he'd use it as an angle to make a complaint if he can spin it the right way. You guys went into Angelo's and caused a scene, witnessed by what might be pack staff, I killed a few trying to find Jamie, and we've been bumping off wolves we think were part of the attack in March left, right and centre . . .'

'Which is why he has a vendetta against you personally?'

'That and I cut off his income stream when we dealt with Evelyn. No one does what they did to people I love and gets away with it. We had our own evidence for each and every single one we went after.'

'Evidence you kept?'

'Of course.' Kia nodded. 'But in some cases, well, we shouldn't have taken it as far as we did.'

Kieran watched her eyes flash.

'As far as . . .'

'As far as Nick took it,' Kia admitted. 'If he has his own evidence of that . . .'

'Ouch.' Kieran ran his fingers through his hair, forgetting he'd tied it back again and accidentally pulling enough free of the hair tie that he had to take it out. 'And now you're hacking bank accounts?' Kieran nudged his chin in the direction of the computer as he ran his fingers through his hair and slipped the tie around his wrist.

'Not really.' Kia grinned. 'Jamie gifted me everything in my mother's name, quite literally. He sent me the files, but since any record of a will has been scrubbed, either in her arrogance or Jamie's tampering, I'm next of kin, it's all mine now anyway.'

'That's heavy.' Kieran huffed out a sigh.

'It's actually fucking handy is what it is.' Kia glanced back at the screen. 'I don't want any of the properties, cars, or whatever else she was sitting on. But these files are golden.'

'Can you do anything with them? Are we as bound by "the rules" as Aiden is?'

'He can't really even know I've got this list,' Kia said, looking shifty before pressing her bottom lip into her teeth with her index finger. 'But, we're not wolves and I'm head guardian . . . so–'

'OK,' Kieran said nodding. 'And Lorna?'

Kia lifted her eyes to his.

'Risky for her to know. But we both know she'll want to help.'

'Of course,' Kieran agreed. 'However, she has enough on right now, let's make a start and involve her only when we need to.'

'Perfect.' Kia grinned.

'Perfect,' Kieran repeated. 'Now go to bed.'

'Excuse me?' Kia looked genuinely blindsided by the command.

'When was the last time you slept? Actually slept, not passed out?'

When Kia was silent long enough to tell him she wasn't sure, Kieran stood up.

'Don't make me throw you over my shoulder and drag you out of this room.'

'OK, OK, take this.' Kia handed him the paperwork she'd gathered and began closing the applications she'd been using. 'Can you take it back to the apartment for me?'

'You're not going straight back there in the morning?'

'I have a couple more places I want to try, then I'll have to start using other methods to find Nick,' Kia admitted sadly. 'But I promise to try and get some sleep.'

Shutting the computer down she stood up to join him and let him lead her up the stairs.

With a quick hug at the door to his room, Kieran watched her drag her exhausted feet to her own room, convinced she'd do as she promised.

EIGHT

'Oh great, you're home.' Kia looked relieved as she fell in the door to find Kieran on the sofa with a beer. 'Have you eaten?'

'Not yet,' Kieran replied, having barely fallen out of the shower and into a t-shirt and sweatpants himself, his wet hair slicked back where he couldn't even be bothered to dry it. 'Are you alright?'

'Fine, fine, I've exhausted all my options . . .'

'And yourself?' Kieran raised an eyebrow and took another swig of his beer.

'I'm working on pure determination at this point,' Kia huffed and placed her fists on her hips as the door closed behind her. 'That and the promise of pizza when Ashlie gets here in half an hour.'

The bottle paused halfway to his lips a second time.

'Girl's night? Shall I make myself scarce?'

'Not at all, I'm hoping to bribe the pair of you with pizza and chicken tenders to start going through that list with me.' Kia glanced around the apartment as she spoke.

'It's on your bed,' Kieran offered. 'Better that than out in the open.'

'Lorna followed you home?'

'Not this time,' Kieran's lips twitched, amused. 'My sister had other things to attend to today, so I put in a cover shift this afternoon to return the favour from yesterday.'

'Vamps?'

'Bingo.'

'How was Aiden this morning?'

'Pissed that you snuck out.' Kieran's eyes darkened. 'Did you actually sleep or just slip out when I said goodnight?'

'I got about six hours before the nightmares woke me up.' Kia shrugged her coat off and perched on the edge of the sofa. 'But nightmares mean he's alive. I think. I know Ashlie's favourite pizza but I've yet to learn yours?'

'Hawaiian,' Kieran deadpanned, unimpressed by the way she was skirting over the facts.

'Seriously?' Kia looked up from her phone.

'No.' He met her eyes, wondering if she'd expand on the nuggets of information. 'Anything with a barbecue sauce.'

'Interesting.' Kia went back to the device. 'Chicken OK?'

'Fine.' He nodded to himself when she didn't look up.

'Right,' Kia announced, tossing her phone to one side and striding into the bedroom.

Closing his eyes and setting his head back and the beer down on the arm of the armchair he was sitting in. Kieran tried to relax as he listened to Kia pick up the papers and put them back down again before moving from the bedroom to the bathroom.

The door locked and the shower was reactivated.

Taking a deep breath, Kieran left his eyes closed and took the time for calm before work was to begin all over again.

'Can you let Ashlie in?'

Hearing Kia in his head even when the shower was still running made Kieran open his eyes and sit up so fast, he almost dropped the bottle.

Before he had chance to frown, the intercom blared into life.

Shooting a look of confusion at Kia's phone, Kieran pressed the release on the front door without moving.

Closing his eyes again, he pinched the bridge of his nose and waited for the elevator to bring Kia's friend to their floor.

'Couldn't you have done it?' Kieran asked, gruffly, when Kia emerged from the bathroom.

'What?' She stopped in her tracks wrapped in a towel.

'If you knew she was here, and you could comms me from in the shower, couldn't you have also pressed the release on the buzzer?'

'Oh, she's here?' Kia grinned.

'Don't act like you didn't know.' Kieran smirked as she disappeared into her room.

When the knock at the door came, he also opened that from his seat, watching as Ashlie let herself in with confusion.

'Don't get up on my account,' she huffed.

'Well, when you don't need to . . .' Kieran offered a shrug even as his lips quirked at the edges at the way she glared at him.

'You'd think a gal wasn't welcome.'

'I let you in, didn't I?' Kieran let the smile form fully, unable to help himself. 'Sorry, it's been a long day and what's the point in having telekinesis if you don't use it every once in a while?'

'Ain't that the truth,' Ashlie admitted with a grudging smile of her own. 'Is she home?'

'Yeah!' Kia yelled from the bedroom.

'Oh good, you weren't shitting me.' Ashlie put her bag down and hung both her own and Kia's coats by the door. 'When she called from the car, I knew she could literally be anywhere,' Ashlie told Kieran.

'Not this time, this is important.' Kia skipped over for a hug with her best friend. 'Thank you for coming.'

'You promised food.' Ashlie waved it off.

'Yeah, pizza's almost here too,' Kia said, grabbing her phone and checking her notifications.

It wasn't long before the pizza and all the sides Kia had ordered had been devoured between them, Kieran finding a new admiration for Kia in the sheer number of hot wings she'd ordered citing that there was "a man in the group".

With sticky fingers, she'd divvied out the list and they'd set to work.

The mission was simple, collect as much data as possible on every name on the list in as ethical a manner as they could manage – to begin with. Kia promised she'd only dig dirty on the ones it was necessary for. That way she was the only one with the severely incriminating evidence, against herself and whatever mutt was in question.

They were sat on the floor around the coffee table when Kia huffed and sat back against the sofa.

'What is it?' Ashlie instantly looked up.

'Bloody vision,' Kia bit out. 'Perfect timing as always.'

'Want one of us to go?' Kieran offered. 'I can go?' he corrected himself, realising he'd volunteered for Ashlie.

'No, it's fine, it should be a quick one, not too far away either. Unless you don't want to be left alone with each other?' Kia shot Ashlie a look, who fired a curious look back at her friend, making Kieran frown.

'I'm sure we'll be fine,' Kieran offered, though it was more like a question.

'Yeah, I promise I'll leave him alone.' Ashlie rolled her eyes playfully, and tucked a strand of hair behind her ear.

Kieran didn't fail to notice that the tips of her ears had gone pink.

'Seriously Kia, pizza night was supposed to be girls' night. I'm not on shift again until tomorrow evening.'

'She doesn't bite.' It was Kia's turn to roll her eyes at Kieran. 'Hard. I'll be back in thirty minutes, tops.'

With that she stood up and tucking her phone in her pocket, left the apartment.

'She's wrong, I do bite hard,' Ashlie said when she'd gone. 'But only when asked nicely.'

Swallowing hard and hoping she didn't notice, Kieran found himself staring at the feisty blonde sat across the coffee table from him. He was suddenly entertaining thoughts of letting her bite him, however hard she liked.

And wondering what type of underwear she might wear.

He gave himself a mental slap and shook his head as he returned to the list on his lap.

'Kia keeps it toasty in here, doesn't she?'

Kieran looked up through his hair at the unexpected comment and found Ashlie tugging her sweater off. It was dragging the vest she had on underneath up over the curve of her waist and threatening to reveal exactly the type of bra Ashlie might wear.

Trying not to groan to himself over how much of a perve he was being, Kieran lowered his eyes again.

Unable to concentrate on the information in front of him, Kieran caught her tousle her hair before fixing her vest, out of the corner of his eye.

'I could do with a break from all this research while Kia's out, fancy another drink?' Ashlie announced as she stood up.

Only she didn't just stand up, she got up in a way that gave Kieran a good look at her cleavage. Straight down the barrel.

With a blink, he finally realised she was doing it deliberately and felt his temperature rise at the thought of "what if."

It had been a long time since he'd entertained the thought of quitting his sleeping-alone habit.

'You can't honestly be that hung up on Kia?'

Jolted out of the frozen-in-place position he'd settled on, Kieran looked up to see Ashlie waving a bottle of beer at his head.

'Excuse me?'

'Oh, come on! She might be too distracted to notice it, but you look at her as though you wish you could solve all her worldly problems and keep her safe from new ones,' Ashlie said, exasperation in her voice as she parked her butt on the coffee table right in front of him.

'Kia knows I don't love her like that.' Kieran frowned up at Ashlie, her breasts a little too close to his forehead as she leaned over him. 'It's been a long time since I've been able to love anyone like that.'

'So you said. Doesn't make it true though.' Ashlie took a swig of her own drink, a cocktail in a can.

'Even if it were true, I'd like my head to remain on my shoulders when Nick returns.' Kieran shook his hair out of his eyes.

'If Nick returns.' Ashlie's eyes flashed and Kieran wasn't sure whether she was suggesting he might be best for her friend or distracted by his own mane toss.

'You think she'll move on if he doesn't?' Kieran asked, knowing they both knew the answer.

Ashlie was silent a little too long. Neither of them wanted to entertain what Kia would do if Nick was gone.

'What you need is a distraction.' Ashlie put her drink down on the table and took Kieran's back off him before sitting on his knees.

'We're supposed to be helping Kia,' he said, dropping the pen and papers onto the floor.

'She doesn't have to know . . . well, she'll know, I threatened to jump you the day I met you.'

'Are you always so forward?' Kieran raised an eyebrow, but his hands found their way onto her knees regardless.

'I know what I want,' Ashlie admitted, her voice soft, taking on a husky edge, making Kieran wonder if she was reigning herself in.

Berating himself for coming across as a lovesick wet blanket for a woman he could never have even if he'd entertained the idea, Kieran decided to run with it.

He couldn't deny that Ashlie had caught his eye. If anything, the interest he had in the woman on his lap had reassured him he wasn't totally dead in the trouser department after all.

Holding her gaze, Kieran silently challenged her to do what she threatened.

Leaning in, Ashlie shifted up his lap until her boobs where against his chest. His hands slid up her thighs to her waist where he toyed with the hem of that vest.

Running her tongue over the dimple in his chin, she moved in to kiss him, winding him with the intensity it carried.

Left breathless and suddenly desperate for more, he stood up, holding her perfectly in place as he did so.

Wrapping her legs around his waist and arms around his neck as he gripped her ass, she let out a yelp of delight at how effortlessly he handled her.

Kieran carried her to his bedroom, kicking the door closed behind him in case Kia came back earlier than planned.

'How do you want me?' Ashlie whispered in his ear before he let her slide back to her feet. 'Fast?'

Biting her lip, she peeled the vest and sports bra she was wearing off together, leaving her breasts free as she reached out to lift his t-shirt up and off.

Once he was bare chested, she pressed her nipples to the firm heat of his chest and kissed him again. This time Kieran held her close, letting the kiss deepen, savouring it.

In that moment, he didn't need to do anything more, he'd have happily spent the twenty minutes or so they had just kissing Ashlie. If he never did anything else with another woman, he'd die happy.

Then she nipped his lip impatiently.

'You're a fucking good kisser Kieran, but we haven't got all night,' Ashlie breathed, kissing him once more before turning her back on him to pull her jeans down and lean provocatively over the bed frame.

'Shit,' he muttered, breathless.

'I want what you've got barely hidden in those sweatpants, and I want it over here, right now.' Ashlie tossed her hair back as she peered over her shoulder.

Shucking the pants off completely, Kieran moved towards her and reaching down, kissed her shoulder, trailing his lips down her spine until he was crouched behind her.

She watched him as he went, curiously.

Helping her feet out of her jeans and realising she too had gone commando that night, Kieran playfully bit her ass cheek before standing up again.

The gasp she let out wasn't of outrage but of rapture as she continued to watch him.

'I just need you to . . .'

Ashlie let out a moan of impatience when he ran a hand up the inside of her thigh, nudging her legs further apart before sliding the hand forward to test the waters. Finding her beyond ready for him, he let his hand inch further still, finding her clit and rolling it gently between finger and thumb.

When her legs buckled with another moan, he gripped her by the hips and gave her his full length.

'Holy shit!' Ashlie cried out, backing into him for more.

When she arched her back, willing him on, he slid his hands up her sides to cup her breasts and tease her nipples.

'Harder.' Ashlie managed between loud cries of ecstasy. 'Harder, Kieran.'

Slipping one hand across her breasts he let the other snake across her pelvis, returning his fingers to her clit and using the pressure his wrist had on her hipbone to hold her in place as his hips did exactly as she asked.

Gripping the forearm against her chest, her nails digging into his skin, Ashlie fell apart with a scream, shuddering against him as he slowed to a stop, kissing the back of her neck when his own release followed.

'You can do that to me any time.' Ashlie's eyes were bright as they snuck across the living room to the bathroom to clean up.

'What about . . . ?' Kieran started awkwardly.

'Oh, don't worry about that, I've got it covered.' Ashlie winked, sitting on the edge of the bath to watch him get dressed before she shut him out of the bathroom.

When Kia returned, she found Kieran and Ashlie lounging on the sofas, more drinks bottles and cans strewn across the coffee table and the list of werewolves neatly stacked and completely red penned.

They both looked up to chide her for being gone for hours, only to stand up in shock at the state of her.

'What the fuck happened?' Ashlie blurted at the same time Kieran asked;

'Are you alright?!'

'Nothing serious, I'm fine,' Kia snarled.

Kieran stepped in front of her when she continued towards the bathroom and Ashlie took a step back. Kia was covered in blood, and what looked like clumps of hairy flesh.

'Kia, I saw Nick come back in that state several times before . . .' Kieran started but felt Ashlie's wince even as Kia's look darkened.

'I was working,' Kia bit out.

'I've never seen Lorna make this much mess.'

Kieran's jaw ticked as he tried to cover the sting from the hair tug Ashlie gave him telekinetically.

'That's because you're too busy working or in your own head to notice much these days.' Kia's eyes flashed, spoiling for another fight.

'Look who's talking,' Kieran fired back knowing then that Kia had no idea how much he'd tried to be there for her.

'Indeed.' Kia let her glare settle on him. 'Do you mind if I clean up before I try to calm down enough to talk about it?'

'Sure.' Kieran jumped out of the way as she moved forward anyway.

Once Kia had locked herself in the bathroom, Kieran turned back to Ashlie, only to find her at his shoulder.

'Do you think she found something?' Kieran asked quietly, his eyes searching Ashlie's face as she stared at the door to the bathroom in the wake of her friend.

Her eyes slowly drifted to his, 'No. Not this time.'

'Why?' Kieran's voice was hushed.

'Because when she does realise she's got to spend the rest of forever trying to work out how the hell she's supposed to live without him, she won't be that calm.' Ashlie's eyes were sad as she gripped his forearm briefly and headed back to the sofa.

Kieran watched her go and wondered how someone who had been so glib about romance the day before could hit the nail so perfectly on the head.

'You think he's dead?' Kieran asked as quietly as he could manage as they returned to the sofa.

'I can't understand how he could be missing without being dead. I thought they were supposed to know where the other is at all times.' Ashlie shook her head sadly and leant against him, her head on his shoulder.

'They also know when one or the other is mortally wounded,' Kieran muttered, his eyes taking on a haunted look as he remembered Kia's own mother shooting her in the chest, and the look in Nick's eyes when he'd landed behind Evelyn.

Ashlie's eyes glistened as they drifted over Kieran's shoulder to the bathroom door. When she looked back, he raised his eyebrows as if to say "exactly."

NINE

'What do you mean you were *forced* to kill one of Cain's pack?' Aiden pinched the bridge of his nose, trying hard not to shout.

'In the circumstances I wasn't given much of a choice,' Kia stated calmly.

'He's calling for blood, Kia.'

'He was calling for that anyway,' Kieran muttered, receiving an elbow to the ribs from Lorna for his trouble.

'Don't you start,' she returned.

Rolling his eyes, Kieran fought off another yawn. Kia's phone had been ringing off the hook before she'd even finished in the shower.

After Kia had admitted the shortened version of her night, Ashlie had gone home to grab some sleep before her next shift in the shelters and Kieran had jumped in the car with Kia to head out to face Aiden and Acheron.

'I was working!' Kia reiterated for the fifth time. 'If I get a vision, I get a vision – admittedly not often for werewolves . . .'

'That should have been your first clue!' Aiden exclaimed, spreading his arms wide.

'They're not officially pack wolves, the rules are a bit different,' Lorna offered. 'But it is unusual.'

'By the time I knew she was associated with Cain, it was too late.'

'She told you?' Acheron looked up from where he had been staring thoughtfully at the floor.

'Well, when she wasn't trying to actually bite my head off, yes, she was quite the talker.' Kia's eyes narrowed. 'Telling me how Cain wanted her to deal with me, that Cain killed Nick . . .'

Aiden sighed heavily. 'Kia, they're using that to bait you. And you fell for it.'

'I'm not stupid, Aiden,' Kia snapped back. 'That wasn't all she said, and as I have just pointed out, she was trying to kill me.'

'You're certain?' Acheron asked calmly.

'What part of "Cain wants me to deal with you," suggests she wanted a tea party?' Kia snarked back.

Aiden went to speak, but thought better of it and pursed his lips instead.

'Couldn't you have avoided making a mess?' Lorna narrowed her eyes at her fellow guardian, knowing what Aiden was thinking.

It was Kia's turn to remain silent as she met Lorna's eyes.

Kieran scowled at the pair of them, and Kia let him into the vision she was sharing with Lorna. It took everything Kieran had in that moment not to swear and give the game away.

The wolf had been determined to tear lumps off Kia.

So, Kia had torn lumps off the wolf, quite literally.

But there was something she wasn't showing the twins, her eyes diverting back to Aiden before the images could get really messy.

'Sounds like one crazy bitch,' Lorna said lightly to break the silence.

'Crazy or on a mission,' Kia shrugged.

'Looks to me like he's breaking the rules already, Aiden,' Lorna stated.

'Neither he, nor his pack are breaking any rules before an official challenge has been made,' Acheron admitted quietly, 'So whatever Kia's run in was about tonight, it can't be used against either pack member. And I use that term lightly on their side.'

'Now who is he trying to rile?' Kia's eyes flashed as she glanced at the phone in Aiden's hand.

'Do you know where this so-called pack is? Or is it spread out?' Kieran asked.

'Sounds like more of a cult than a pack,' Lorna scoffed. 'And you let him challenge you.'

'I'd rather we knew when they were coming. If he pulls a stunt like last year, our casualties could be vast.' Aiden barely refrained from glaring at Lorna.

'We already expected him to come back for another shot. We won't be caught so unawares next time,' Scott said as he walked in from the kitchen where he'd been eaves dropping with a few of the other wolves who had been in search of a midnight snack.

'No,' Aiden agreed. 'But our numbers are down. I'd rather he came for me first. And for Saracen to be prepared to take you in.'

'If he wins, he's not just going to let us walk across the city to the O'Neill's,' Joey pointed out.

'He's right, Aiden,' Dante confirmed as Seth put the last of his sandwich down, looking a bit green. 'Besides, it's not the rest of this pack he seems to have a problem with, it's the core Barnes family and the fact that we welcome non-wolf members.'

'His involvement with my mother — fuck, I hope it was purely business — will have given him a front row seat to what was happening with Nick,' Kia said.

'He won't have liked the way we were hunting down the members of his pack that we could track either,' Dante continued. 'His words in this room said as much. He saw what Nick was capable of, what Kia is capable of. Acheron and I know he hates protocol and hierarchy, that's why he had to leave in the first place. But he knows enough about it to use it against us.'

'Some pack this is going to be if he succeeds,' Seth mumbled.

'I'm not planning on letting that happen.' Aiden sat back in his seat. 'Nick may not be around, but Cain has to come to me first, and that's how I want it.'

'Let's just hope he doesn't use this issue with Kia to play dirty then, Pup,' Dante said as he turned on his heel to return the plate he'd been picking from to the kitchen.

'Why do you think I told him I don't control Kia?' Aiden said before Dante could leave the room.

Dante's eyes slid from Aiden, to Kia, to Acheron.

'We've already lost two of our strongest fighters,' Dante pointed out darkly. 'Let's try not to lose anyone else, shall we?'

Seth jumped up to join his father in the kitchen before they both headed to bed.

'Now what?' Scott asked.

'Now nothing.' Aiden sighed. 'We have to wait. Kia, did you contact cleanup and file a report.'

'Of course,' she drawled.

'OK, so I don't even have to reply to him. He can check with the registry.'

Kieran was staring into space in the direction of the kitchen. Dante's words resonating with him.

They'd lost Nick, they'd found Danyl, Kia had been attacked. It wasn't math Kieran liked in the slightest.

'What if he picks off anyone else?'

'We can't be certain that's what he's doing.' Aiden's voice was tight with frustration.

'*Make sure he's not*,' Lorna transmitted to Kieran and Kia.

'If anyone else goes missing Aiden, *I* will kill him,' Kia bit out and cut him off before he could berate her for it. 'Especially if it happens before papers are served.'

Without waiting for an answer, she left the room.

Watching her go, Aiden merely raised an eyebrow when she actually went upstairs and didn't just stalk out of the house.

'It's probably time we were all in bed,' Acheron offered.

'Yeah,' Aiden said on a sigh as Scott and Joey followed Acheron out.

'Go on up,' Lorna gave Aiden a light shove in the direction of his father as he stood up. 'I need to talk shop with Kieran.'

'HQ stuff?' Aiden pulled a face. 'Sure.'

'Rude.' Kieran smirked. 'Couldn't get him out of the place when I got back.'

'It's not that, he's trying to stay focused, so I'm keeping the other two hats I wear to myself.' Lorna inclined her head in the direction of the kitchen and Kieran followed her to where she pulled up a stool at the island, cracking two bottles of beer from the fridge as she went.

'Don't you dare tell me you need me to keep an eye on Kia.' Kieran accepted one of the bottles with a grin that told her *nice try*.

'I wouldn't dream of it,' Lorna widened her eyes with mock-innocence. 'I know you can't work and keep track of her the way she is right now. I need to ask you a favour related to what you do though.'

'That, I can handle.' Kieran nodded. 'I will also check in with Kia when I see her.'

'Thank you.' Lorna also nodded, turning her beer bottle in circles on the counter in front of her. 'Have you had anyone present to you in the medical unit with needle marks, deep cuts they can't explain or bites?'

He'd been in the middle of drinking from his beer, but as it soured in his mouth, Kieran put the bottle down and swallowed the mouthful with difficulty.

'I haven't. But I can ask. Why?'

'There has been a sudden downturn in the trend for biting guardians, so I don't actually expect you to find bite marks . . .'

'Well, that's a relief. Finally. But?'

'Declan said there are some vampires off radar, and he's concerned.'

'And you believe him?'

'He's been very responsive to this whole process, he wants the veil of mistrust lifted from his kind too,' Lorna said evenly. 'He's concerned there are vampires out there who have found another way to get their hands on guardian blood – and that they're the ones holding on to Hillary.'

'He's convinced she's alive?'

'Seems to be.' Lorna nodded without breaking eye contact with her brother. 'Though he is playing his cards very straight.'

'He wants leadership.'

'I confess I don't know enough about their rules to know whether he's being shady or not. But I'm trying to learn.' It was Lorna's turn to smirk. 'He should never have let me inside the consulate. There's so much info.'

'I'll ask tomorrow night when I'm on shift. I haven't seen anything suspicious, but someone else might have.' He ran his fingers through his hair in thought. 'If there is some blood farming still going on though, underground guardians could be the target.'

'I don't want to trouble Kia with that right now.'

'It's OK, we have others we can ask to use their connections.' Kieran grabbed the beer, the earlier part of the evening coming back to him suddenly, and drained half the contents in one go.

'Ashlie?' Lorna arched an eyebrow, but amusement played on her lips.

'If she's around here or if I bump into her at HQ I can ask.' He offered a shrug. 'But Mia will know a few guardians who are ex-underground, I'm sure.'

'Only if the opportunity arises. We don't want her alerting Kia.' Lorna nodded.

TEN

Sitting up in the dark, it took Kieran a moment to process the screaming coming from down the hall and to realise his phone was ringing at the same time.

Hearing Lorna run from her room, he grabbed for the phone when he saw it was Mia.

In the end the two were completely unrelated and ten minutes later he was stood in the entrance hall of the pack house in his jogging bottoms, staring out at the flying dust Kia had created as she'd made a swift retreat.

Lorna was leaning out of the front door, having attempted to run after Kia.

Aiden appeared beside Kieran and handed him a cup of coffee, a hastily thrown-on pair of jeans unbuttoned and hanging precariously from his hips, which Kieran pointedly ignored given they'd all flown out of bed.

He was just glad his sister was dressed.

'Thanks,' Kieran muttered, able to smell it was pure espresso before he'd raised it anywhere near his lips.

Lorna stood back from the door and turned to see Aiden watching her.

'Go after her if you feel you need to,' he said evenly.

'We don't know why she left to know where she went,' Lorna finally spoke, her face pale from the echoes of those screams. 'Besides, she flew.'

'She what?' Aiden blinked through the threatening yawn.

'Yeah.'

'That's not good, right?' Kieran asked quietly.

'Lorna said Mia called you.' Aiden stole a glance at Kieran. 'Has something happened?'

'That was completely unrelated and bad timing.' Kieran shook his head. 'Hence the need for the coffee, emergency cover down at HQ.'

'What was she doing down there at this time of night?' Lorna glared out at the dark wintery driveway.

'It's not that early. She sometimes goes down to use the gym before work.' Kieran shrugged and drained the last of his cup. 'It just feels middle of the night because we just got to bed late.'

There was a moment of silence as they all tried to find the words to ask each other about why Kia might have reacted the way she had. In the end Kieran made a move to head back up the stairs.

'Keep me updated, I'll try to keep an eye on my phone. If you need me urgently, call Mia or Ben.'

'OK.' Lorna offered a nod.

'Did we ever find out what Ben's meeting was about by the way?'

'Declan fighting for control.' Lorna shrugged. 'We assumed right. But he's getting pushy.'

'Just what you need at the moment.' Kieran rolled his eyes at his sister. 'I'd better get moving.'

Leaving Lorna and Aiden to debate their next move or head back to bed, Kieran went to the kitchen to refill his mug before taking his second caffeine hit to his room to gulp as he got dressed.

Mia had promised him a shorter shift if she couldn't get his team to re-organise his night shift.

It was going to be a long day.

And not just because Kia had driven them over and his bike was at the apartment.

'Take mine,' Lorna said dangling her car keys in his face as he left his bedroom.

'Breaking into my sleep-deprived brain to see if I know where Kia went?' Kieran arched an eyebrow as he gladly took the keys. 'Thank you.'

'Something like that. Also checking my big little brother is OK.' Lorna looked up at him, 'You look exhausted.'

'Nothing a month of sleep wouldn't fix when this is all over,' he said with a smile as he hooked an arm around her neck to drag her in for a hug. 'And by *this* I mean the training.'

'That was your own stupid idea,' Lorna teased from within his bear hug.

'Don't I know it.' He ruffled her hair as he let her go. 'I'll check in as soon as I have a moment. What are you going to do?'

'What can we do?' she yawned.

'Go back to bed for at least . . .' He glanced at his watch, 'Another two hours.'

'Yessir.' Lorna offered a salute as they parted ways, her for her room, him for the stairs.

'Lorna's gone back to bed. I don't think there's anything more you can be doing right now. Kia might just be working,' Kieran said to Aiden, who was still at the open front door as he reached the bottom of the stairs.

'I've never heard her scream before going out on a vision.' Aiden dragged his eyes from the driveway to look at Kieran.

'Neither have I. Let's just hope she's OK. Whatever she saw.'

Offering another nod, Aiden moved to the side to let Kieran out and silently closed the door behind him.

Jumping in Lorna's Escalade he took a moment to try Kia's phone. He knew she wouldn't answer, but he couldn't let her leave without letting her know they were there for her if she needed them.

He just hoped a missed call was enough to convey the message.

ELEVEN

'How on earth did you do this?' Kieran peered at the inch deep gash he was trying to clean.

Seeing through the blood was proving tricky, so he grabbed an ice pack and slammed it over the wound, receiving an angry hiss for his trouble, and reached around to the tray behind him for the stitch kit.

'Hold that,' he instructed. 'You need stitches.'

'What else is new?'

As Kieran turned from the bed the patient was perched on to the table the tray was on to drag it closer, he saw a familiar figure wander up the corridor through the open door.

Scowling to himself and checking the clock, he shook his head.

'It's a clean cut at least.' Kieran appraised as he regained control of the ice pack.

'Meaning?'

'Whatever was in your way – whether it was put there by another's hand or not – must have been bloody sharp.'

'I wouldn't know.'

'Oh?' Kieran's hand paused, needle in hand.

'I don't remember it happening.'

'What were you fighting?'

'Does that matter? It's dead,' the guardian harrumphed.

Relaxing at those words, Kieran set about stitching the unwanted incision.

The figure crossed the doorway again.

Kieran glanced at the clock again, and sped up his needlework.

Five minutes later, the inconvenienced guardian was tugging her t-shirt back down over her patched up hip.

'Thanks. Guess it was too deep to heal quickly on its own after-all.'

'That's what we're here for.' Kieran offered a tight-lipped smile as she shrugged on a jacket and headed for the door.

'Oh, and it was a vampire.'

'Sorry?' Kieran frowned.

'A vampire ran at me as I was hog-tying a demon for the registry to collect.' She shrugged and flipped her white pixie-cut out of her eyes, stuffing her hands in her pockets. 'It's dust. But I didn't realise I was wounded until I got to the bar, so yes, I guess it had to be a very sharp implement.'

With that she left the room and Ashlie slid into it.

'Any news?'

'Hi Ashlie, how was your day, great to see you,' Ashlie mocked.

Kieran stared at her for a moment too long.

'What?' Her face paled.

'Have you heard from Kia?'

'Not since last night. Why?'

'She bolted from the house with a scream.'

'Fuck.'

'Understatement.' Kieran placed his hands on his hips.

Ashlie dug into her pocket and retrieved her phone. A few taps and swipes and she held it out to Kieran.

'She's at home.'

'How can you know that?'

'When we were both Underground, we had a pact to track each other if we hadn't heard anything in a while, so we could find each other. Dead or Alive. Apparently neither of us thought to delete the tracker.'

'Handy.' Kieran nodded. 'OK, well Mia hasn't dragged me out of here either, so I assume she's checked in with Lorna and all is fine.'

'When do you get off?'

'Three minutes ago.' Kieran sighed and ran his hand over his head making Ashlie smile and recognise it as a tick from before he had hair long enough to tie back.

Reaching up, Ashlie gently tugged his hair out of the bun he'd hastily thrown it into.

'May I walk you to your phone?'

'If you wish.' Kieran smiled. 'Weren't you at the Shelters today?'

'Yeah, eight till four. Then I popped in here for a workout.'

'You've been in the gym?' Kieran glanced back up the corridor in the direction of the facilities.

'Not yet,' she admitted and dragged him into one of the doctor's sleeping quarters as they approached the locker room.

Sticking her head back out into the corridor to make sure the coast was clear, she slid the occupied sign into place and locked the door.

'You really are very direct when you want something.' Kieran was right behind her when she turned.

'Not just anything.'

'Tell me.' Kieran's eyes challenged her as his voice deepened.

'Kiss me.'

'Where?'

'Everywhere.'

Kieran held her gaze for a moment while they both imagined all the places he might kiss her.

'Where will you st–'

Silencing her by kissing her on the mouth, Kieran paused only briefly.

'It's only polite to start with your mouth,' he hushed with a smirk as she caught her breath.

'Trust me to pick the gentleman.' Ashlie rolled her eyes playfully.

'Damn, the bad boy biker facade just fell from your eyes? I thought that was really doing it for you,' Kieran arched an equally playful eyebrow.

'Oh, it was,' Ashlie teased, placing her hands on his chest as he leant over her, one arm casually crooked against the wall. 'I guess we'll just have to play doctors and nurses instead.'

'You want a pair of scrubs?' A mischievous glint reached Kieran's eyes as he glanced at the cupboard in the corner.

'Can we?' Ashlie followed his line of sight as she balled a handful of his shirt in one hand.

'Let's see.' Kieran moved to the cupboard and looked inside. 'Ah, not in this room it seems.'

'Damn.' Ashlie bit her bottom lip thoughtfully. 'You'll just have to strip.'

'I've been in these all day,' Kieran reminded her.

'You better smuggle me a pair for next time then.' Ashlie's eyes widened with a grin.

'I can do that,' Kieran agreed as she moved back into his arms.

'So where were you?'

'On my way down.' Kieran matched her grin before attacking her throat with heated kisses to distract her long enough that he could manoeuvre her onto the bed.

She pulled back as if to lie down, but Kieran held her in a sitting position as he got to his knees between her thighs and proceeded to remove the sweater she was wearing.

Finding a t-shirt underneath, he trailed kisses up her arms before removing it.

As he threw the t-shirt on the bed, she found a moment to grab the back of his collar and tug the scrubs shirt over his head, which was less ceremoniously dropped on the floor.

Taking a moment to appreciate the way the black lace of her bra supported her assets Kieran first nudged one nipple into life with his nose before gently taking it between his teeth.

'Kia was wrong, you're the biter,' Ashlie managed between hitched breaths as he repeated the process on the other nipple. 'Ironic really.'

'Shh,' Kieran commanded, kissing his way across her chest, continuing to tease both nipples through the flimsy lace as he started tugging her trousers down.

'Don't shh me!' Ashlie said with mock outrage as he dragged all the clothing on her lower half down past her knees, kissing her stomach as his head travelled south, his hands parting her knees once the clothing was pooled around her ankles.

'You want the whole complex to hear what I'm about to do to you?' Kieran peered up at her from between her thighs, his voice husky, one eyebrow arched in challenge.

'I . . .' Ashlie was about to shoot back that she didn't care either way, but Kieran slid his arms under her legs to grip her hips as he planted his mouth around her clit. 'Shit!'

Kieran chuckled, sending shockwaves through her body and causing her to grip the bedding to steady her upper body.

Every part of her below the waist belonged to Kieran until he was ready to let her go. Which he was forced to do when the bed suddenly ignited at her fingertips.

Leaning away from the flames, he reached for her hands to put out the fire, only to realise she was falling backwards.

Managing to smother fire before it could completely scorch the bed, he also had to telekinetically catch Ashlie before her head could connect with the wall.

'Ashlie?!' He jumped up to sit on the bed and lift her into his arms as she started to regain consciousness.

'Wow,' she cooed dreamily.

'What the hell happened?!' He looked from her dazed and glassy eyes to the ruined bed cover, sporting two charred circles where her hands had been.

'You tell me,' she muttered, still barely coherent.

'You burnt the bed,' Kieran stated. 'And passed out for a moment.'

'I burned the bed?!' Ashlie sat up. 'Whoops.'

'Do you often pass out during sexual activities?' Kieran frowned, the concern etching itself on his brow.

'Nope, that's a new one,' she smirked wistfully. 'Going to be a pain in the ass if it means I miss half the orgasm though. More of those please.'

With a smile she reached up and ran her fingertips over his jawline before shifting onto her knees.

'So where were we?'

'Take it easy for a moment, you just blacked out.' Kieran shifted so that he was facing her.

'I'm fine,' she huffed, glancing over her shoulder at the state of her ankles where her clothing still pooled. 'Oof, maybe not.'

'Just take a moment,' Kieran offered reaching out to pull her onto his lap.

Silently, Ashlie settled her torso into his arms before bringing her knees up and fixing her clothes.

'Are you warm enough?' he asked.

'I should probably get dressed,' Ashlie mumbled reaching for her t-shirt.

As she redressed, Kieran called the scrubs shirt to him and put it back on.

'I should probably check in with Lorna and Kia, see if there's been an update on Nick.' Kieran smiled as Ashlie fixed her hair around her sweater.

'Kia's at home. She'd have gone to the pack house if it was dire, surely?' Ashlie met his eyes.

'Can we be sure of that?' Kieran offered her a twisted smile.

'Good point, you'd better get home then,' Ashlie said evenly.

'You're not coming with me?' Kieran asked as he opened the door.

'She doesn't need me in her face as well. Besides, I've got a date tonight.' Ashlie shrugged as she walked through the door he held open for her.

'Right,' Kieran said simply, trying to keep his own voice level to hide the pain her barbed words, intentional or not, had caused. 'Well, you know where I am if you need me.'

'Yes. I do.' Ashlie turned with a devilish grin and sidling up to him reached up to kiss his chin and run a hand down his chest.

Kieran reached up to play with the curls resting on her shoulder, but she was gone before his fingertips could make it, leaving his hand hovering mid-air.

'Right,' Kieran said again to the corridor as he turned and headed for the locker room.

TWELVE

Letting himself into the apartment, Kieran prepared himself for battle. He didn't expect Kia to want to talk to him, and he hadn't expected to find the apartment dark.

Lorna had left him a message to say Kia had checked in as working, but that it had all gone quiet since.

Moving to the kitchenette, he kept his eyes on Kia's bedroom door, it was open, but he couldn't quite see whether there was anyone on the bed. The bathroom door was closed, but there was no light showing from beneath and it had been dark for hours.

Opening and closing the fridge with a bang, he paused, listening for signs that she might be moving around the dark, despite knowing it would be incredibly hard to hear her either way.

'Kia?' he called, tentatively, and popped the cap off the beer he hadn't put in the fridge.

A shiver of dread rolled down his spine as his eyes were drawn back to the bathroom door.

'Kia, are you home?'

Beer forgotten, he began moving towards the bathroom.

Trying the door, he found it locked.

Without allowing the unwelcome thoughts to settle in, he telekinetically unlocked the door and peered inside.

'Kia? Are you OK?'

It took him a moment to spot her, given the bathroom, like the apartment, was in darkness. What he spotted first were her knees which were just visible over the top of the tub.

Rushing to the bath, throwing the light on as he went, he found her torso submerged in murky water. It wasn't full red, but there was definitely blood in the mix.

With a loud, 'Fuck!' he reached in and dragged her out onto the floor.

She wasn't breathing but she had a pulse. Assessing her for injury, all he found was some nasty bruising around her ribcage.

While his mind began spinning, considering internal bleeding, broken ribs, a head injury and accidental drowning, his body went onto autopilot, instantly administering respiratory assistance in the hope of clearing any water from her lungs.

She remained unresponsive for longer than he was comfortable with, but as he rolled her onto her side she convulsed, spewing out a bucket load of bath water.

'Breathe Kia!' he yelled at her.

Throwing several towels around her as she returned to a state of consciousness, gasping, coughing and retching as she expelled the last of the water, Kieran held her close to warm her up, her fingertips blue with cold.

'You're OK, it's going to hurt for a bit, but you're OK,' he soothed as they leant back against the tub, sat in a puddle of water.

'What happened?' Kia asked quietly after taking a moment to calm down.

'You tell me.'

Biting back a growl of pain against the bruising, Kia attempted to shift herself and gave up almost instantly.

'Another vision gone wrong,' she said after a moment, her brain getting over the shock of almost drowning. 'The blood isn't mine, I didn't mean to pass out.'

'Even if it would have been fucking convenient?' Kieran said darkly.

'How do you figure that?' Kia bit back, managing to turn her head to glare at him.

'That scream you let out this morning was inhuman.'

'It doesn't mean he's dead.'

'Oh really?' Kieran snarked in disbelief.

'It means someone's torturing him,' Kia collapsed in his arms again, going floppy with a hiss of pain as tears began running down her nose. 'At least that's what the nightmares are telling me.'

Rubbing some warmth into her arms, Kieran mumbled, 'OK. We'll go over that later, how long do you think you were in the tub?'

'Got in around three this afternoon.'

'Kia, it's eight p.m., that's not possible.'

Kia's sobbing paused with a surprised hiccup. Even the taste of blood and soap it brought with it couldn't distract her from the facts.

'I should be dead.'

'Yes, you probably should. Luckily, it seems you didn't slip under straight away,' Kieran bit out.

'If I think he's still alive, it's not like I did it deliberately,' Kia snapped back.

Tipping her head back so that her neck rolled over the edge of the bath she took in the state of the water.

'What is that?'

'Mud mostly, I told you the blood isn't mine.'

'I could see that at least,' Kieran agreed.

'I might need you to check my ribs in a moment, I think I broke a couple.'

'A couple?!' Kieran spluttered a laugh. 'Judging by the bruising, you broke most of them.

'That would explain the pain.' Kia gasped as she tried to move again. 'That water's gross, I need a shower before I let Doctor Titan near me again.'

With a smirk she shifted across the floor slightly, but squeezed her eyes closed against the pain as she moved.

'The doctor has seen worse,' Kieran said, offering a smile, 'How about some wicked-strength painkillers before you attempt that?'

'Ooh, yes please.'

'OK, are you alright while I go get them? I'll clean this up while they kick in.'

Tucking the towels around her, expecting her body temperature to have been dangerously low given how long she was in the water, Kieran rushed from the bathroom to ransack the kit in his room. He was back in seconds, making sure she took the maximum dose before he helped her move to the wall, away from the bath so he could get the room cleaned up.

'If you need to sleep, you're going to need to give me permission to get you clean and into bed,' Kieran warned her after glancing over and finding her lids heavy.

'You dragged me from the bath, I doubt there's much you haven't seen at this point.' Kia glared up at him.

'Kia, I'm a medic, I'm not coming on to you,' Kieran sassed, resisting the urge to roll his eyes at his latest patient. 'At the very least you can tell my sister on me.'

'Good point,' she muttered back.

'Right, let's get you standing before I let you anywhere near the shower.' Kieran moved across the bathroom and held his hands out. 'Do you have the strength to telekinetically hold the towels where you want them?'

'I think I can manage that.' Kia nodded and shrugged off all but two, keeping one around her shoulders, the other around her waist.

Reaching out to clasp his hands and let him help her up, Kia screamed as soon as the tension moved through her torso.

Kieran set her back down again quickly.

'No,' she ground out through gritted teeth, 'I can take it, just get me to my feet.'

'This might feel a little weird, but it's something we've been trying with patients. I'm going to use my telekinetic energy to support your body all over and lift from all angles at once. It will feel like you're off balance, but I won't let you fall,' Kieran promised with a squeeze of her fingers.

'OK, go for it.' Kia nodded.

Within seconds, but with a loud yell, Kia was on her feet. Kieran maintained a similar hold to support her as he'd used with Danyl while she got her breath back.

'You're right, that is weird.' Kia looked down and around herself. 'But oddly soothing.'

'I'd say you've done a bit more than break a couple of ribs.' Kieran appraised the bruised skin as she revealed the areas that hurt the most.

'Like what?' Kia looked up a little too quickly and ground her teeth again.

'You might have ruptured something, maybe your spleen,' he told her, glancing up briefly to find her watching him, 'But that could also have killed you in the time you were in here.'

'What are you saying?'

'Aside from that you're really fucking lucky, there probably isn't much I can do by now. You'll have healed a great deal on your own in that time. Surgery would be pointless, by the time I got you down to HQ and ran tests to be sure, there would be very little left to repair. Doesn't mean the surrounding tissue isn't going to hurt like a bitch for a few hours more though.'

'Lucky me.'

'What actually happened?'

'I was wrestling a shadowdancer.'

'Not your brother, right?'

'No, not Jamie. I was trying to keep him out of the darker spots of a roof I'd chased him to. Something . . . I got a secondary vision, but it was more like one of my nightmares . . . threw me off long enough for him to drag both of us off the ledge.'

'How far?'

'Fifteen stories.'

'The shadowdancer?'

'Pancaked.'

'You walked away?'

'It knocked me out first. And I waited for cleanup to arrive and scoop him up before I attempted to move too far.'

'You really should be dead,' Kieran stated, his voice hollow as his brain tried to work out how she was standing, mostly on her own, in front of him. 'Why did you wait for clean-up? I'm surprised they didn't haul you into HQ for examination.'

When Kia was silent a moment too long again, he was able to answer for her.

'You needed to use Nick's demon wings to get back here.'

She nodded sadly.

'They just appeared after one of the nightmares. I don't know what that means.' Kia shrugged and winced in regret. 'I can't always control them.'

'Kia . . .'

'I know, I know, it's not good.' She rolled her eyes to the ceiling. 'But it's also why I believe he's still out there. Somewhere.'

'Do you want some help with this shower, or do you feel the painkillers kicking in?'

'I think I can manage . . . you perve,' Kia teased.

'Medic,' Kieran repeated as professionally as he could manage.

'I bet you say that to all the girls.' Kia grinned as she took sliding steps towards the shower.

'Not as many as you think want to play dress up with the doctor these days,' he returned with a playful smile.

'Oh, I can think of at least one who'd jump you if she got the chance,' Kia said, distracted by the slow movements she as concentrating on.

'Would that be your friend Ashlie?' Kieran glanced over his shoulder as he headed for the door.

'Ashlie doesn't usually hang about when she sets her sights on a target.' Kia laughed, the sound carrying a fondness for her friend. 'She might be just what you need to kickstart your return to dating. Not that she really does dating.'

'What do you mean?' Kieran paused, his hand on the doorframe.

'She homes in on what she wants and can't be bothered with the trial-and-error method of traditional dating. If she does take you for a test drive it will most likely only be the once. Just enough to get you back in the saddle, if you know what I mean?'

'Yeah, I know what you mean,' Kieran said with a smirk, knowing they were already beyond the you-broke-it-you-bought-it stage and wondering what Ashlie would do with him next.

One thing was for certain, if Kia's words were correct, there was no date.

THIRTEEN

While Kia showered, Kieran kept himself handy, returning to the beer in the kitchen and thumbing through the contacts on his phone as if Ashlie might suddenly message him.

Not that they had ever exchanged numbers.

He wondered what she was really doing as he glanced over his shoulder at the bathroom door, closed but unlocked in case Kia needed him.

Kieran also toyed with the idea of letting Lorna know Kia was hurt.

Then decided his life wouldn't be worth living in the short term if he did. He'd rather Lorna tore him off a strip further down the line. He was too tired, and too wired to deal with that sooner than he needed to.

When his phone rang, he groaned.

'Stop that,' he growled at his sister.

'You know how this works by now, right?'

'You know that you're the one who insists we keep out of each other's heads, right?' Kieran sassed back.

'Harder when you're tired,' Lorna admitted gently.

'Sorry,' Kieran said on a sigh, realising she was right.

'What's up?' Lorna asked quietly, her tone telling him she was moving to somewhere she would be alone, so he got up and moved to his own bedroom door.

'Pick one,' Kieran replied quietly.

'It's OK, you can tell her.'

Kieran looked up to see Kia gingerly moving from the bathroom to the bedroom.

'I'm going to just get some sleep.' Jerking her thumb over her shoulder as she disappeared into the bedroom a haunted look in her own eyes where her brain had clearly caught up with what had happened to her. And what might have, or should have, happened to her.

'Kia had an incident earlier this evening,' Kieran told Lorna as he moved into his bedroom to sit on the bed in the dark, beer once again forgotten.

'Vampire?'

'Nothing like that.' Kieran contemplated lying on the bed, but knew he also needed a shower before he gave himself a chance to nod off. 'She was distracted during a vision and had an accident that should have killed her.'

'Sorry, what?'

'She thinks something is torturing Nick.'

'Thinks?' Lorna pushed.

'I think she *knows* something is torturing him, and it's affecting her. I think she must feel it.'

'Why hasn't she told Aiden?'

'Maybe because he won't listen?' Kieran paused. 'Or doesn't want to hear it. That's his brother, and he's got enough going on right now.'

'Shit,' Lorna whispered to herself. 'What else?'

'That's all I've got.' Kieran shrugged, despite knowing she couldn't see him.

'Bullshit,' Lorna replied.

'That's all she'll tell me.'

'I don't mean her anymore. What's up with you?'

'I'm just tired.' Kieran sighed again.

'Tired enough that I'm vibing something else,' Lorna said softly. 'Are you OK?'

'Yeah, don't worry, it's nothing.' Kieran closed his eyes but opened them again when Ashlie's face swam behind his lids.

It was just a couple of hook-ups.

Fuck the fact that it was the closest he'd been to another being in years.

'Do I need to give the sibling talk to anyone? I hear that as ex-head guardian, and part vamp, I can be a scary ass big sister.' Lorna grinned down the line.

Kieran rolled his eyes with a fond smile. Nothing in his love life got past his sister. It never had.

'Seriously, I'm fine. It's really nothing.'

'It's not . . .'

'Fuck off, Lorna,' he growled.

'OK, not her. What changed?'

'I told you it was never like that. I'm just . . . well, you said it yourself, I lead a lonely existence sometimes.'

'Hits harder when you're already run down,' Lorna agreed. 'Maybe take a few days off?'

'I'll see what I can do,' Kieran offered, knowing that if he really let himself feel it, he'd gladly sleep for a week. 'Any news from the mutt?'

'Aiden's meeting with Saracen in the next couple of days, but nothing from Cain yet,' Lorna answered.

'Alright. You know where I am if you need me.' Kieran winced, remembering saying those exact words to Ashlie.

'Too true. I can also swing pack business with Mia if you want that time off,' Lorna reminded him.

'Ah yes, so if I want out of stitching the wounds of clumsy guardians, I can come out there and wait to be snapped at by a moronic furball,' Kieran groused playfully. 'Speaking of which, I had one tonight who needed stitches after a vampire tried to cut her mid-vision. He wasn't even her target.'

'You think it could be what Declan was afraid of?'

'Maybe. The guardian in question dusted the vamp rather than ask questions, but whatever the weapon, it was very sharp, so it wasn't looking to bite – and it wasn't in a place that would kill her fast. The potential for a bit of blood-letting was there I think.'

'Great,' Lorna said bluntly. 'You'll need to let Kia know. I'll ask Mia to put out a bulletin and warn the girls.'

'We could get Asha and Luca to keep an eye out for incidents we might not hear about otherwise.'

'Good plan, especially if you're going to get a few days out,' Lorna mused. 'Right, get some sleep.'

'Another good plan,' Kieran said, yawning down the phone at her, causing her to yawn right back. 'Good night.'

'Night. Love you,' Lorna said gently, her concern bleeding through her voice.

'Love you too,' Kieran replied, just as softly, with a smile.

FOURTEEN

When Kieran fell out of his room the following morning in a blind panic after being woken up by a vision, Kia almost dropped her drink.

'You OK?' her soft voice asked from the sofa.

Finding Kia sat curled around a cup of tea, Kieran finally took a breath.

'Vision, erm, can you track Ashlie?'

'I can.' Kia arched an eyebrow and took in the state of him again, dishevelled in a pair of black jogging bottoms and a tight t-shirt of the same colour.

'Where is she?' Kieran began hopping into his sneakers.

Suddenly realising the panic wasn't just from being woken up, Kia put her mug down and bolted for the bedroom to collect her phone.

'What's happened?'

'I don't know, something about a vision of hers about to go wrong.'

'OK. You might need to explain a few things to me on route, but I need you to take a breath, maybe splash your face with some cold water, and focus,' Kia said as she tapped at her phone.

'Are you in a fit state to leave the apartment?'

'I feel amazing.' Kia shrugged. 'Besides, that's my best friend you're in a fluster over, so I'm coming with you whether you like it or not.'

Kieran stood straight and for the first time noticed that Kia was fully dressed and moving about as though nothing had happened.

'I might not be the only one needing to answer some questions.' Kieran placed his hands on his hips.

In doing so, he felt the material of the joggers, and peering down at his attire, swore, and headed back into the bedroom to swap the flimsy cotton for a pair of jeans. By the time he reappeared, Kia was at the door, her own sneakers on.

'Ashlie's a big girl, she can handle herself you know.' Kia glanced at Kieran as they rode the elevator down to the parking garage.

'I'm sure she can, but this vision . . . it was weird, I don't know why we need to get to her, we just do.'

'Now you're scaring me.'

'Believe me, you're not the only one.' Kieran raked his fingers through his hair.

Neither of them had bothered with a coat in their haste, knowing their own energy shields could provide all the warmth they would need.

'We can drive to Shelter Two, dump the car and zip over to the park she's stopped in.'

'Was she due at the shelter this morning?' Kieran finally glanced at his watch.

'Maybe, I can't remember all her shifts,' Kia said, looking sheepish, 'But that would put her nearby.'

Kia held her phone up to show Kieran the green dot that was Ashlie, moving very slightly around the edge of a fountain.

Nodding, he felt his stomach sink for reasons he couldn't explain and a new form of panic sweep over his shoulders.

Equally as unsettled by his behaviour, Kia let the silence sit between them until they reached the park, even letting him drive her car like a lunatic without a word and keeping quiet when he drove all the way to the park and dumped the vehicle on the sidewalk.

Running to the fountain, Kia a few steps behind him, Kieran skidded to a halt to find Ashlie sat on top of a telekinetically cuffed vampire.

'Are you OK?' Kieran asked her, but wasn't looking at her, he was too busy scanning the rest of the park's occupants.

'I'm fine. What the fuck are you two doing here?' Ashlie glared up at Kieran but noticed Kia was also turning circles like she was looking for something. 'What is it?'

'Did your vision go OK?' Kia shot a look back over her shoulder.

'Yeah, I was just about to read this moron his rights, nothing unusual.' Ashlie bounced on the back of the vampire, causing a hiss of annoyance. 'He was antagonising a werewolf, and I was just reminding him that's against the rules.'

'What?' Kia's scowl turned to bafflement. 'That's a stupidly minor offence for a vision.'

'Tell me about it, but I was told to go, so I go.'

'No one move,' Kieran muttered suddenly and threw a shield around them all as three werewolves broke cover from various trees and bushes and ran at the guardians.

The vampire even had the decency to swear loudly and try to run for his life.

Ashlie zapped him to remind him to hold still, even as they all watched in awe as the werewolves barrelled into the shield full force.

Barely bouncing back from the blow, all three paused to growl at the guardians before making a run for it.

'That was weird,' Kia stated, her eyes narrowed as she watched the three mutts disappear into the distance.

'Bit more than fucking weird. Is that why you're here?' Ashlie was watching the retreat over her shoulder.

'I guess so.' Kieran finally dropped the shield, feeling the threat that had woken him up dissipating at last.

'You guess so?!' Ashlie glared up at him.

'Um, can I go?' the vampire wriggled again.

'Know what you did wrong?' Ashlie barked down at him.

'Y-yes,' he squeaked.

'Then yeah.'

'Wait.' Kia turned on the vamp as he got to his feet.

Ashlie reached out and grabbed him by the collar.

'Which werewolf were you antagonising?' Kia sauntered over, leaning up into his face, despite the height difference.

'The big grey one. Can I go now?' the vampire huffed.

'Sure.' Kia's eyes narrowed as she watched him leave.

'Recognise any of those fleabags?' Kieran asked Kia when they all finally felt their collective guard relax.

'Not specifically.' She shrugged. 'Probably just wanted another pop at the dude before we let him go.'

'Or at least we hope so.' Kieran raised both eyebrows pointedly.

'You don't think so?'

'No, I don't think so.'

'Excuse me refusing to do a damsel routine, but what the fuck just happened?' Ashlie forced her way between her friends.

'A vision woke Kieran up this morning,' Kia said.

'For those asshats?' Ashlie motioned in the direction the wolves had run.

'No,' Kieran admitted, his jaw tight. 'For you.'

'Me? I was perfectly fine.' Ashlie turned a hardened stare on him. One that told him she'd prefer to chew his head off than thank him.

Shaking his head, Kieran walked off. Though he made sure he stayed in earshot.

'The vision told him something was about to happen to you,' Kia explained for him.

'Isn't that a bit strange?'

'He had it with Lorna once, might just be part of how his visions work.'

'Ah.' Ashlie tried to look as though she understood even as she shot a glance in Kieran's direction. 'You don't think that was just a twin thing?' she hushed.

'If it was, how would he know you might have a werewolf problem today, and why would he scramble to get down here so fast?' Kia shot her friend a look.

'Scramble?' Ashlie dragged her eyes back to Kia.

'Practically fell out of the bedroom when the vision woke him up.'

'He gives a shit about a fellow pack member.' Ashlie shrugged and diverted her eyes from her friend's gaze.

'Ash . . .' Kia folded her arms. 'What have you done?'

'I merely followed through on the threat I made.'

Kia sighed and, closing her eyes, pinched the bridge of her nose.

'Twice.'

'Twice?!' Kia's eyes flew open.

'SHHH!' Ashlie grabbed her by the arms and pulled her out of Kieran's vision.

'You never go back for seconds.'

'He's . . .'

'Ash, he's like a brother to me, and he's been through a lot.' Kia cut her off before she could offer sordid details

'Fuck. I know.' Ashlie bit her lip guiltily. 'There's something else.'

Grabbing Kia's wrists, Ashlie leaned in and whispered in her ear.

'Right,' Kia said slowly.

'That's all you've got to say on the matter?' Ashlie's eyes were wide.

'The rest you'll have to figure out for yourselves.' Kia grinned with a look at Kieran as he began making his way back to them.

'Kia tell you about her night last night?' Kieran asked, folding his arms as he drew to a stop beside them.

'No,' Ashlie looked between them suspiciously. 'Lunch?'

'You two go, I'm going to go see what my sister wants.'

'Lorna twinned you?' Kia smiled.

'No, she messaged me, like a good twin should.' He shot them both a pointed look. 'Enjoy your lunch.'

Watching them head for Kia's car, he took a moment to check his bearings.

'Need a lift?' Kia called over her shoulder.

'Depends on which direction you're heading in,' Kieran said, falling in step with them. 'I need to get to Broomstyx.'

'Haven't you seen enough of that place lately?' Kia looked up at him, dragging his eyes away from the back of Ashlie's head.

'Not enough for Lorna apparently, though she is talking about getting me some time off.' He rolled his eyes.

'We'll drop you, it will give us time to think up a suitable lunch venue.' Kia smiled.

'Thanks. And over lunch I'm sure Ashlie can tell you how her date went last night.' Kieran smirked knowingly at Ashlie when her head span almost one-eighty to glare at him.

'Oh, I'm going to want to know all about that.' Kia grinned.

'It was cancelled.' Ashlie waved it off, regaining her composure.

'Wait, what?' Kia stopped in her tracks. 'I thought you meant . . .'

'You know what, I'm going to walk, let you two get some quality girl-chat.' Kieran narrowed his eyes at Ashlie as he turned and walked away before either of them could argue, wishing he could stay to hear that discussion.

He glanced back only once to see Kia prodding Ashlie for answers while Ashlie stared after him in disbelief. Though there was a smile in her eyes he didn't fail to notice.

FIFTEEN

'Feel better?' Lorna asked, expertly dodging Kieran's left hook.

'Getting there,' he admitted, reaching out and hooking that arm around her neck to drag her down onto the mats where they retrieved their water bottles and sat in sibling companionship for a moment.

Having walked to Broomstyx, Kieran had been ambushed by Mia, Lorna and Asha. One look at Kieran and Asha, at Mia's request, ratted him out and announced how tired he really was, causing Mia to cancel all his shifts to the end of February.

It wasn't worth protesting that taking five weeks out of training wasn't ideal. It was already agreed. With the caveat that if there was an incident, he could volunteer.

That left him fully at Lorna's mercy and after running him home to repack another bag, she'd taken him out to

MaryVaille, ordered him to get a kit on and meet her in the gym.

Using her forearm to wipe the sweat from her forehead, Lorna watched her brother carefully.

'What?' he asked, side-eyeing her.

'Who you screwing?'

'Wow.' He took the final mouthful from his bottle before shaking his head in disbelief. 'Blunt as ever.'

'I suspected as much. You were off on the phone, now, seeing you . . .' She shrugged.

'It doesn't matter.'

'Someone at HQ?'

'Never you mind, I'm pretty sure it was a once-ish off.' Kieran returned the shrug.

Scooting up next to him, Lorna leaned against him while she finished her water. Kissing her sweaty temple, he offered her a nod and they continued to sit quietly.

'We'd better get cleaned up. Saracen O'Neill is due for dinner tonight,' Lorna said after a moment.

'The O'Neill alpha?' Kieran asked as he got up, gripping her by the hand to pull her up with him.

'That'll be the one. I haven't met him yet either.' Lorna waggled her eyebrows at him as they moved across the basement gym.

'Explains why there are a number wolves in the house.' Kieran rolled his eyes and began following her up the stairs to the main entrance hall but she stopped and turned back to him.

'Any woman who beds my brother and doesn't instantly fall in love with him is a fool.'

'I'm sure that's very wrong – on a couple of levels,' Kieran scowled, 'but I appreciate the sentiment.'

'Well, I think you're a catch, for the right person. But I'm biased.' Lorna hugged him tight, wrapping her arms around his torso.

With a fond chuckle, he squeezed her just as close.

'If you weren't on my team, I'd be right on track to become a miserable old bastard,' Kieran said lightly.

'Become?!' Lorna teased before bolting up the stairs away from the expected swipe but Kieran didn't move, which caused Lorna pause at the top of the stairs.

'We both know I have my moments,' Kieran admitted.

'You've always had your moments.' Lorna smirked. 'You can't help it.'

Rolling his eyes again, Kieran caught up with her. 'Yeah, yeah.'

Coming out of his room, showered and changed a little while later, Kieran glanced down the corridor to see Ashlie watching him before collecting herself and disappearing into another room.

Passing Nick's room on his way to the stairs, he found Kia tossing a bag onto the bed as well.

'Saracen's visit is a big deal then?' Kieran asked, pausing.

'The reasons for it tonight are. But generally, we do touch base with the O'Neills more often than you'd think,' Kia explained as she threw on a hoodie Kieran knew to be Nick's and joined him at the door.

'How have you been?'

'I told you, I feel fine.' She looked up at him. 'I know I really shouldn't, even on a guardian's repair settings.'

'It is odd. Any more nightmares or visions?'

'No. But I took Ashlie scouting with me this afternoon, see if I could feel any more in some new search areas.'

'Where have you moved the search to?'

'After this morning . . .' Kia glanced up and down the corridor and over the banister to see if anyone was in earshot. 'We tip-toed around the edges of Cain's neighbourhood. It's not that far from the park.'

'Can you do that?' Kieran hushed back, slightly alarmed.

'Not technically, no, but we know most of his pack reside in the northern quarter of the city. Cain himself lives in a hotel penthouse.'

Cutting herself off as more wolves let themselves in the front door, Kia peered into the hall again.

'Did you get leave?'

'Lorna's cleared me until the end of February . . . what?'

'What is it with the end of February?' Kia hissed, looking like her words might have been more choice than that.

'Nick's birthday?'

'Yeah.' She glared down at Aiden as he crossed the entrance hall to meet the new arrivals. 'He's told me he'll hold a memorial if he's not back by then.'

'Shit.' Kieran glanced down at Aiden too and raised a hand in greeting when he looked up.

'I might need to borrow you, if Lorna allows.'

'Sure.' Kieran glanced back at Kia. 'Recon?'

'Yeah, something like that.'

Nodding, Kieran began heading downstairs. Kia didn't follow, he noticed, she headed for Ashlie's room instead.

Realising everyone, including Aiden had moved to the dining room already, that's where Kieran let his nose lead him.

'Kieran.' Aiden appeared next beside him as he entered the room, the table already half-full with wolves, his sister lounging next to a disturbed chair he assumed to have been Aiden's. 'Before you sit down, this is Saracen O'Neill.' Aiden gestured, introducing the man sitting directly to his chair's left.

Saracen stood up, his hand outstretched as Kieran found himself looking up, even at little over six feet himself. True to the Irish roots of his family name, Saracen's curly shoulder-length mane was a dark auburn, though his skin tone defied his ancestry with a gentle olive tone from a Spanish-born mother. His dark brown eyes surveyed Kieran from top to toe with unguarded curiosity.

'Saracen, this is Lorna's twin brother.'

'Ah, the other Titan, I've heard a lot about you.' Saracen's deep voice held a chuckle and he paused long enough for Kieran to begin to feel uneasy. 'Not all bad I promise you.'

As he released Kieran's hand, Kieran shot a look at Aiden, who merely grinned. Of course the alphas had discussed Kieran's initial disgust at his sister's choice of co-worker and eventual bedfellow.

'Headstrong woman your sister. Just what Aiden needed to keep him in check.' Saracen nodded in Lorna's direction.

'Tell me about it, I grew up with her,' Kieran offered in return as he took the seat she'd been saving for him on her other side.

Resting her hand on his shoulder, she offered a squeeze of reassurance.

Finding Oakley and Ramsey opposite, Kieran decided to make polite conversation until he was needed.

'This whole process is making me edgy as fuck,' Ramsey bitched. 'I can't take the waiting.'

'How do these things usually go down?' Kieran asked, reaching for a jug of water on the table and filling his glass.

'Usually with the burial of an alpha,' Oakley deadpanned. 'He's just trying to scare us, he didn't make a song and dance of announcing his arrival when he attacked last March.'

'Arguably, that was to deplete numbers and hedge response prior to this,' Kieran offered.

'History tells us that challenges for leadership were most often made in the heat of the moment, though the rules remain basically the same now that we have the Registry to keep an eye on proceedings, once a challenge is thrown it has to be carried out within days and it's always to the death,' Oakley continued. 'Since the Registry came into force there have been fewer such challenges, mostly because taking the time to file the notice offers enough time to rationalise the flare of anger that prompted it.'

'Given Cain has clearly been thinking about this for decades, I think he's way beyond any kind of cooling off period.' Ramsey rolled his eyes and drained the wine glass in front of him. 'More wine?'

'Sure, and if you're going to keep downing it like that, we'll need a few more bottles.' Oakley looked pointedly to the bottle. 'Let's go grab some more.'

As the couple left the table, Dante leaned over to interject for Kieran's benefit.

'There are plenty of packs around the world who would still rather tear each other to shreds over territory.' He sniffed to show his distaste for it. 'But that's their business.'

Nodding, Kieran watched Kia and Ashlie walk in, engrossed in conversation. Curious, Kieran tried to eaves drop but they were drowned out by the general chatter around the room. They seemed to be talking Shelter business, so he tuned back into what his sister was saying.

Aiden and Lorna were talking about how Saracen would be involved in the upcoming skirmish.

'Aiden says you'll be on hand when Cain makes the challenge official, does Cain know that he has to inform you so you can be available?' Lorna paused for a response, but the doorbell rang, and all present pack members knew they didn't need to request entry. 'No fucking way.'

'That would suggest one of us has a leak,' Saracen said quietly. 'That or he's watching pack members or the house a little too closely.'

When Lorna, Aiden and Saracen stood, so did Kia and Kieran.

Sure enough, on the front steps, waiting patiently this time, Aiden found Cain, Sean and two unknown wolves.

Peering through the party in the hall towards the dining room Cain stepped through the door.

'Sorry to break up the party.' He smiled, his eyes flicking to Saracen briefly. 'But we have business to attend to.'

'Alright, we'll use the living room.' Aiden nodded and motioned for Cain to follow him.

Kieran took the back end of the party and noticed Saracen step behind Kia when one of Cain's wolves looked ready to move in. She pursed her lips when he placed a hand on her shoulder to let her know it was him. She merely nodded in response.

Kieran pushed the front room door mostly closed behind him for privacy as he entered last. When Cain gave him an obvious once-over, he merely glared back as Davide, Saracen's second sprang into the room, slightly late on the uptake.

'So, you've come to set a date?' Aiden asked Cain as everyone found a seat.

Everyone except Kia.

'Does she have to do that?' Cain shot Kia a black look.

'Stand by the door?' Kia asked innocently. 'No . . . I can stand behind you if you'd prefer?'

'No, I think I prefer *you* to be where I can see you.'

'If you believe that makes you safer, sure, I'll stay here.'

'Kia,' Aiden warned with a smirk.

'You encourage her. I won't be so lenient,' Cain warned.

'Should this pack fall, Kia is spoken for,' Saracen interjected.

'You can't do that,' Cain bit out.

'You've just openly threatened her welfare, I bloody well can, and I will, furball.' Saracen grinned. 'Though it would be interesting to see exactly how you plan to discipline the head guardian.'

Kia's eyes fell on Saracen as he maintained eye contact with Cain. She was itching to show them all just what she'd do if Cain went anywhere near her.

'Guardians have no jurisdiction here,' Sean pointed out.

'Not whilst part of the pack, unless I give them permission. And they have my permission to assist this pack and its members however they deem necessary. If you think Lorna and Kia will be at your disposal once I'm gone, you're very much mistaken,' Aiden informed him.

'Does that protection include you?' Cain questioned him.

'No. Your challenge is our business, just you and me. But if you set the rest of your wolves on the rest of this pack they will defend each other to the last. This pack is a family.'

'How touching. But then, all families have their crazies.'

'If your problem is really with the brutal way in which non-wolf members of this pack handled some of your strays last year, then I doubt you have much case for a challenge.' Aiden pursed his lips.

'What Nick was capable of was carried out under your instruction. The same goes for any other pack member who acted like a monster,' Cain pointed out.

'And who gave your mutts permission to rip this house apart last march? By your own statement, you too should be guilty of such atrocities,' Saracen said calmly.

'You can't prove that.' Cain shrugged with a smirk. 'But I will bring the wolf back to this pack. No more happy families.'

'There won't be much of a pack left if you take it by force.' Saracen's eyes bored into Cain's.

'Well of that I'm certain, non-wolf members will be expelled or dealt with for starters.' Cain's eyes moved from Kia, to Kieran, to Lorna who he lingered over in a manner that made her flesh crawl.

To cover for the grimace she wanted to display, she merely leant forward.

'You won't get anywhere near me,' she cooed and when he smirked, opening his mouth ready to say what his eyes had already told her, the wolf nearest him suddenly clutched at his throat, his mouth opening and closing desperately as his face turned purple.

Aiden lay a hand on Lorna's to lace their fingertips together and she let the wolf go.

'We'll see about that.' Cain glanced at his subordinate as he regained his composure and got to his feet as soon as the colour returned to the wolf's face.

Glancing from Kia to Aiden as Aiden also stood, Cain withdrew a letter from his coat pocket and handed it to him.

'You have until the twenty-eighth.'

'Of course we do.' Kia rolled her eyes as she folded her arms and leant back against the wall.

'Those are my terms.' Cain returned his attention to Aiden, who was reading the letter, Saracen having got up to look at it, was peering over his shoulder.

'Yeah, it's all here.' Aiden looked up as Cain and his team prepared to leave. 'Except where your wolves will be at the time.'

'They'll be here.'

'That isn't standard procedure,' Acheron pointed out.

'I've afforded you the luxury of coming to you, the least you can do is afford me a little protection if anyone gets out of hand.' Cain side-eyed Kia.

'If you're worried about foul play, I suggest we do this on neutral ground,' Aiden offered.

'Sadly, you can't.' Saracen sighed, locking eyes with Cain. 'It has to be on the territory of the pack under challenge. The worm doesn't even have to let you know where his *pack* is based. I've read the rules too, I'll be here.'

'We can mitigate for that.' Aiden shrugged.

'I'm guessing this *family unit* will be on hand to bury you?' Cain looked again at Kia. 'Including that.'

'Call me what you want. Just like Lorna, I don't have to touch you to kill you. Remember that.' Kia blew him a kiss as the door opened at her command. 'See you at the end of the February.'

'I trust you'll stay away from us until then.' Cain addressed Kia but met Aiden's eyes and checked Saracen's features.

'If I have reason to see you before, I'll be *working* that day.' Kia shrugged.

'Kia, he's granted us legal channels, you must offer him the same,' Aiden warned.

'We really would need to be naughty boys and girls to cause a vision after all.' Cain pouted at Kia as he turned away from Aiden. 'Without one I think you have to tow my line.'

'Best behave yourself then, hadn't you?' Kia's eyes flashed as she moved away from the wall and strolled past Cain to head back to the dining room.

'You have a real problem with that one,' Cain told Aiden as he showed him to the front door.

'Don't make her yours too then.' Aiden shrugged and closed the door behind the quartet.

'Why aren't the dragons here?' Saracen asked Aiden as they all turned away from the front door.

'That's a good question.' Lorna stopped in her tracks. 'They said they'd be here in case he showed.'

'Want me to check in with Mia, see if something's come up at the bar?' Kieran asked, reading his twin's mind.

'Could you?' Lorna nodded.

'I'll be back in a minute.' Kieran patted his pockets and

headed for his room.

SIXTEEN

'Do you need me down there?' Kieran asked Mia as he sat on his bed with the phone to his ear.

'I don't think there's any more medical care we can give at the moment, and neither of them will leave the facility until he's shown signs of improvement.' Mia promised. 'They'll be safer here.'

'Shit,' Kieran breathed. 'Alright, I'd better go and tell Lorna.'

'OK. I did try to get hold of her an hour ago, but her phone must be off.'

'Probably in her room. We've had a situation here ourselves.'

'That's suspicious,' Mia stated.

'Tell me about it,' Kieran agreed before signing off and heading back to the dining room where everyone was sedately working through bowls of curry.

'Either you guys are taking this challenge a little too calmly, or you've heard?' Kieran asked, returning to his seat, finding Lorna had set a bowl of food ready for him.

'We're mostly just processing. Heard what?' Kia offered.

'Get some food Kieran, you must be famished,' Sookie suggested with a gentle smile from the end of the table nearest the kitchen.

'Yes. Thank you, Sookie.' Kieran nodded but knew he had to continue. 'Asha and Luca were attacked as they left Broomstyx to head out here this afternoon. Asha is shaken up, Luca is quite broken.'

'How broken?' Kia dropped her fork, ready to get up, Lorna froze next to him.

'Bones mostly, but they're keeping them down at HQ while they make sure there's nothing internal going on. Safety in numbers there too.'

'What mugged them?' Ashlie asked when everyone else seemed too stunned to.

'Werewolves,' Kieran said quietly.

'Son of a bitch,' Lorna slammed her cutlery down. 'Aiden, we should get down there. Make sure they're OK.'

'Surely he's broken his own sanctions, Aiden!' Kia glared across the table.

'Timelines suggest it was before he came here to deliver the letter,' Aiden said, though his voice was hollow.

'What if he did it to get you two out of the house?' Ramsey was wide-eyed.

'Just Lorna and myself will go. We'll set the security system to max,' Aiden said, getting up.

'Aiden, it's Luca, I need to go.' Kia also stood.

'I need you here Kia, please.' Aiden met her eyes.

'OK,' Kia agreed, all reluctance falling from her manner at the tone in his voice.

'*Will you stay too?*' Lorna asked Kieran who nodded in return.

'*Of course.*'

'We should leave,' Saracen announced.

'No, don't feel you have to, stay and finish your meal at least.' Aiden turned to the other alpha. 'I'm sorry I need to go.'

'Perfectly acceptable in the circumstances.' Saracen waved him off. 'We'll grab a drink before the twenty-eighth, get each other up to speed.'

'Thank you.' Aiden lay a hand on his shoulder for a moment before Saracen reached round for a handshake.

With the mood suddenly even more sombre, Lorna led them from the room.

The silence that fell on the room as the front door closed behind the couple and the locks were set was cloying, and as hungry as Kieran felt, he needed a moment before he could take another bite.

'Is there anything we can do?' Ashlie broke the silence first.

Kieran had been watching her fidget next to Kia and wondered if she was uncomfortable with being locked in, or the chance of being attacked. He'd stilled his mind by reminding himself that Aiden had just been thrown an official to-the-death challenge.

And he'd accepted.

'Stay vigilant.' Dante was the only one to speak when no one else did.

'That's all?!' Ashlie glanced at Kieran for another outsider's reaction.

'We're less likely to be caught by surprise that way, but he's set an official challenge, he can't touch us until that date.' Scott offered a warm smile to their newest member.

Kia snorted.

'Just because Aiden has left the building, Kia . . .' Acheron warned, even though Saracen had looked set to remind her also.

'What if Cain isn't really interested in owning the pack?' Kia laced her fingers together under her chin and tilted her head in Acheron's direction.

'Why would he . . .'

'To throw us off looking for him, because Aiden is playing by the rules?' Kia challenged and looked at some of the faces around her to see if they could work out what she was saying, knowing Nick would have said it days before. 'It's bad enough being caught unawares, but what about when you believe you're safe?'

Some forks clattered to plates in realisation as appetites fully disappeared up and down the table.

'Speak to Aiden when he gets back. But as Dante said, we should remain vigilant.' Acheron offered her the slightest nod.

Kieran looked to Kia and Ashlie and knew they were all thinking the same thing. Aiden should never have accepted the challenge.

It was going to be a bloodbath either way.

'I'll keep my pack on high alert too,' Saracen promised. 'And on that note, I really should be getting back.'

Kia got up to run around the table for a hug from the O'Neill alpha before he headed off and ended up walking him to the door with Acheron. The front door could be isolated from the security system for evacuation, but that didn't mean she was going to let Acheron be the only one at the door.

Kieran glanced over his shoulder, wondering what they'd be talking about out of sight, but scrubbed his hands over his face and got to his feet to help Sookie when she started clearing plates.

'Kieran, sit back down!' Sookie chided, but not without a smile.

'Too late.' He grinned as he began piling stacks of bowls in his arms and followed her into the kitchen. 'Now, put me to work.'

She opened her mouth to protest and Kieran saw the tired resignation in her eyes as she nodded towards the sink and row of dishwashers.

He knew the pain of losing both parents, but he couldn't imagine how she felt with one son missing and the other served with the letter Aiden had in his pocket.

'Shall I get my marigolds from my bag?' Ashlie was suddenly in the room with them. 'The werewolves want to discuss serious, morbid matters, so put me to work too!'

'Sure, why not.' Sookie smiled.

'Sookie, let us handle this. I'll bring you a cup of tea in the den if you need a moment.' Kia had also appeared from nowhere.

Turning to Kia, Sookie nodded and the pair slipped into a reassuring squeeze of a hug. When Sookie left the kitchen, it was through the door to the hallway, and she barely looked back.

Kia made the tea while Kieran and Ashlie collected and stacked the rest of the dishes, and ran it out to the den before rejoining them.

'Right,' Kia placed her hands on her hips. 'We ready to do this guardian style?'

'If you turn this kitchen into something out of a children's cartoon, we'll break something. Behave,' Ashlie giggled.

'That would have worked if we hadn't been distracted.' Kia pouted.

'I take it you two have tried this before?' Kieran arched an eyebrow, glancing over his shoulder from the sink.

'College,' they said together.

'We were drunk, and thought we could telekinetically pour cocktails from across the room.' Ashlie smirked.

'Yeah, that doesn't end well. Even when you're not drunk.' Kieran smiled fondly.

'It just needs more practice.' Kia shrugged.

'Not when you and your twin are eleven years old and using your barely-honed skills to sneak ice cream sundaes out of the kitchen from the next room,' Kieran laughed.

'Sundaes?' Ashlie looked impressed.

'We were adventurous kids, but by the time we'd dropped the chocolate sprinkles, broken a bowl . . . Luckily Mum caught the bottle of syrup with her own energy before we sprayed her. Talk about busted.' Kieran smiled at the memory. 'We couldn't even run away, she bound the pair of us from where she was until she'd put the bottle down.'

'Must have been a very talented guardian,' Ashlie whimsied softly.

'Yeah, she was.' Kieran nodded.

SEVENTEEN

With the washing up in hand, Acheron and Dante had taken the wolves into the lounge where conversations had continued, though by the time the guardians and Sookie decided to join them, they'd moved on to drinking.

The lounge contained an antique cabinet full of a variety of whisky and brandy and so they waited for Lorna and Aiden to come home with an update.

When they did, and the questions had simmered down, Kieran found himself up against the corner of one of the sofas with his sister tucked under his arm. When they were teens, Lorna would often fall asleep curled against him on the sofa after a movie night. That she was still happy to grab his arm and wrap it around her shoulders every now and then let him know she was content.

Keeping Ashlie in his peripheral as he spoke with Acheron, Aiden and Lorna, Kieran wondered if she was taking exceptional interest in Scott deliberately.

Kia had left the room after getting the update on Asha and Luca and trying to tell Aiden her thoughts on the challenge. He wasn't in the mood to discuss it and suggested they talk in the morning.

With other things to consider, Kieran was finding it all too easy to ignore Ashlie. He wasn't interested in playing games. If it was just sex, fine, but if she wanted to know how he felt beyond that, she needed to ask him. He waited until most of the conversations ran out of steam before heading to bed.

'Run in the morning?' Lorna asked as he was leaving the room.

'You insist I take time off and then expect me to get out of bed in the A.M.?' Kieran shot her a bemused raised eyebrow.

'Run whenever you get up then?' Lorna rolled her eyes.

'Alright.' He nodded as he left the room.

Scrubbing his hands over his face, Kieran made it to his bedroom on autopilot before flopping onto the end of his bed. It had been a long day.

It was going to be an even longer month.

He wondered if Kia would be allowed to keep looking for Nick and whether she'd gone to bed or snuck out. It was tempting to go to her room and let her offload, but after realising he'd nodded off somewhere between crashing onto the bed and suddenly hearing Lorna and Aiden head into their room across the hall, he acknowledged it was too late for that.

He didn't know which room Ashlie was in for sure, so he couldn't go creeping down the hall.

Shaking his head and stripping down to his boxers he walked into the ensuite and caught a look at his reflection in the mirror as he cleaned his teeth.

Damn he did look tired.

There was no time for romance.

Not when his sister needed him.

Not when half the pack could be dead in a month.

'You look as though the weight of the world is on your shoulders.'

He'd heard her tiptoe into the room, the tiniest of tiny clicks at the door and closed his eyes to take a steadying breath. Lorna, if she was still awake, would have heard that.

And he was sure she'd assume it was Kia.

'It isn't?' Kieran looked to the ceiling when he did reopen his eyes.

Anything to prevent him looking at Ashlie in her sleep shorts and cropped t-shirt.

'You can't save everyone,' she said gently.

'Won't stop me trying,' he replied gruffly. 'Especially when it comes to my sister.'

Ashlie stopped short, as though her surroundings had shifted into technicolour.

'You still think I'm obsessed with Kia too,' Kieran stated, feeling agitated.

'You practically ran home to check on her last night.'

'You're the one who lied about going on a date to get away from me.'

'How do you know about that?'

'Kia grassed you up. Accidentally.' Kieran folded his arms. 'You don't date.'

'I don't see the point.' Ashlie shrugged. 'I told you. I know what I want.'

'Fine.' Kieran's eyes flashed in challenge. 'Is that another flaming orgasm, or did you have a different reason for creeping in here?'

The way her eyes blazed, he expected her to slap him and leave the room. When she did neither, he felt his shoulders lose some of their tension.

'I wanted to thank you for this morning, especially after the revelations of this evening.' Ashlie glanced at the floor, her cheeks reddening. 'And after I was so rude.'

'Forget it,' Kieran said gently. 'We're a pack, which I never thought I'd say to anyone, but it's true, it's what we do.'

'Still.' Ashlie shrugged again.

'You could have told me that at any time.' Kieran stepped closer to her. 'So, I'll ask again, why are you creeping into my room in the dead of night, dressed like that.'

'It seemed more sensible to bring it up in private.' Ashlie met his eyes and held his gaze.

'Oh really?' Kieran raised both eyebrows. 'You didn't want anything else?'

'I'm not here to make demands, not this time.'

'Well, no, next time I think it should be my turn. But . . .'

'But what?' her voice shook.

'You don't do next times.' Kieran shrugged nonchalantly and stepped back.

'What would you do to me if I did?' she asked quietly, her eyes dilating as she took in his almost-naked form in front of her.

'That would be telling.' Kieran smirked and turning the bathroom light off began moving towards the bed. 'Night, Ashlie.'

'No.'

Turning he found her right behind him.

'No?'

'Show me.'

'Seriously?'

'Y-yes.'

'I'm not going to be rough with you. Not this time,' he warned.

'OK.'

'Is it?' Kieran took her chin gently in one hand and slid his thumb over her bottom lip.

'Uh huh,' Ashlie mumbled as his head drew closer to her mouth, his other hand gliding up her side, under her t-shirt, that thumb tracing the underside of her breast beneath.

When their lips met, Ashlie sighed into him, pressing the warm skin of her midriff into the heat of his torso. Her hands slid up his back, memorising the contours of the muscles at his shoulders as the kiss deepened.

Kieran slid the hand cupping her chin back, his fingertips tracing her jawline before he entangled them in her hair, gently keeping her where he wanted her as he prolonged the kiss.

While he had her in his arms, that's where he hoped to keep her for as long as possible.

Chest to chest, they moulded together in a way that felt too right to be a fling. But he wasn't stupid enough to force something that wasn't meant to be.

That didn't mean he couldn't savour every inch of soft skin she was willing to let him touch.

Manoeuvring them both so that he could sit on the end of the bed, he settled her on his lap.

Pausing only to remove her t-shirt, Kieran pulled her close again, causing a pout when she realised he wasn't going to play with her breasts, at least not yet.

'Patience,' he murmured against her mouth before expertly gripping her by the thigh and turning in a way that put her beneath him on the bed before she knew what had happened.

Fighting to keep quiet and let him get his revenge, Ashlie closed her eyes and drank in every caress as he explored her body with both hands and lips as she lay on his bed.

At some point the rest of their clothing disappeared, but she couldn't have told anyone who asked when, just that her shorts were replaced by his hands, stroking and caressing every inch of her and when he dipped his fingers inside her she wasn't sure how she didn't fall apart there and then, her eyes opening only momentarily to see the look of satisfaction on his face.

His mouth remained a slave to her breasts while his hands took her to the brink of ecstasy.

Despite herself, she couldn't hold back a tiny whimper when all contact suddenly stopped. Peering through her lashes, wondering where he'd gone, she found him looking down at her from where he lay next to her.

'Still with me?' he whispered, his eyes alight in the dark as he reached out to trail circles across her stomach with his fingertips.

When she nodded, he reached over to kiss her mouth, sucking gently on her bottom lip as he shifted on the bed, settling himself between her thighs and entering her fully in one long slow stroke.

When a moan began in her throat, he met her tongue hard with his to stop her.

Feeling her arch beneath him, Kieran shifted, making her feel his full length down to her toes and catch her breath.

She reached for his shoulders but he clasped her hands in his and pinned them to the bed, ready to put out any fires either of them were about to create as his hips found a deep, steady rhythm.

When she began showing signs of reaching her peak, he deliberately slowed down until she settled, pushing her to the edge several times before he let her come, shuddering and exhausted beneath him as he found his own release.

'Well, that showed me,' she looked up at him through the haze of afterglow.

'Payback's a bitch.' He grinned as he returned to her side, pulling the covers around them against the night air.

'At least we didn't burn anything that time.' Ashlie held her hand out in front of her, wriggling it free of the burrito he'd turned her into with the blankets.

'Just as well.' Kieran tucked a pillow under his head. 'Setting off the smoke alarms really would have rumbled us.'

'I should probably go back to my own room,' Ashlie struggled to say through a yawn.

'Plenty of time for that,' Kieran said, fighting a yawn of his own and closing his eyes.

Expecting her to bounce as soon as his eyes were shut, Kieran was surprised to hear her breathing deepen. Peering back across the bed, he found her asleep.

He listened to her breathing until slumber took him.

Kieran woke at dawn to Ashlie sneaking back into the bed.

'Back for fourths?' he mumbled through sleep.

'Get over yourself, I just went to the bathroom.' Ashlie sniggered as she bundled up in the covers. 'It's bloody cold out today.'

With a quiet chuckle, Kieran reached out to scoop her up.

'Don't fight it, it's warmer this way,' his said, his eyes closing again and voice full of sleep as she wriggled into little spoon position.

'So much for sneaking back to my own room.' Ashlie winced when the sounds of footsteps and doors opening and closing reached them from down the hall.

'That's your problem.'

'How do you figure that?' Ashlie trailed her fingertips up and down his forearm in front of her.

'I'm not the one in the wrong room. In my underwear.' Kieran smirked to himself thinking how he'd have kissed her shoulder if she hadn't put her clothes back on. 'And your room is on the other side of the house.'

'Fuck,' she whispered, mostly to herself.

'What if they start looking for you?' Kieran asked, his voice was light, but he felt her stiffen in his arms.

'Kia knows where I'm likely to be.'

'Ah.'

'You don't sound shocked by that.'

'Besties talk. And besides, you told me that first time you'd already told her you'd jump me given half the chance.'

'Good point.'

'If I've had my three strikes though, we can work out a way of getting you out of here.'

'Oh?'

'Claim a medical complaint.'

'A guardian, claim a medical complaint?'

'You said you're clumsy.'

'You're right, I did tell you that.' Ashlie glanced back over her shoulder, making him give up on sleep and prop his head on his palm to look at her. 'Do you have any bandages in here.'

'All the better to tie you up with,' Kieran sassed before sobering. 'Yes, if that's the angle you want to play.'

Letting her go, he climbed out of bed and headed for a kit bag he'd stashed in the closet once Lorna had confirmed he could keep the room.

'So Miss . . .'

'Ashford.'

'Your name is Ashlie Ashford?' Kieran couldn't help the smile that crept onto his face as he sat beside her.

'Yes.'

'And when exactly did you disown your parent's Miss Ashford?'

'Erm,' Ashlie fixed her gaze on his face to prevent from looking at him fully naked in the morning light, 'I'm still working on that.'

'So, what's the ailment today?'

'Does it matter?'

'It does if you want my lies to align with yours.' Kieran waggled his eyebrows. 'Please ignore the fact that the doctor is naked Miss Ashford, or he may be tempted to commit an act of malpractice.'

Letting her eyes travel to the part of him she was becoming increasingly fond of, Ashlie grabbed a pillow and covered his lap with it when they heard the door to Aiden and Lorna's room open and close.

Kieran watched the back of his bedroom door until what he was sure were Aiden's footsteps had headed towards the stairs.

'I burned the back of my hand making a cup of tea.' Ashlie lay her wrist on the pillow in front of him, gently, hyper aware of what it was hiding.

'OK.' Kieran nodded, moving his attention to strapping her hand.

When he was finished, he lifted her hand by the fingertips and gazed her knuckles with his lips.

'Whatever you need,' he said, his voice low.

Nodding, Ashlie got to her feet. She waited by the door until he'd thrown on a pair of black jeans.

When he joined her, she reached for the door, but paused for a moment.

Meeting his eyes and finding them questioning, she placed her hand on his chest and kissed him softly, quickly, and then she was opening the door.

Only to find Lorna opening hers at the same time.

Kieran flew into action.

'I'll check it again in a couple of hours, but it's not that bad a burn.'

'I'm such a Clutz.' Ashlie rolled her eyes at Lorna, holding up her bandaged hand. 'It's handy having a doctor in the house.'

Kieran expected Lorna to look relieved that the woman in his room wasn't Kia, instead, the look she gave Ashlie would have wilted flowers.

To her credit, Ashlie kept her head high as she returned to her room as though she'd never even met Kieran before that morning. Even though he knew it meant he was likely never to ever see Ashlie naked again, that she could turn her back on his sister's death-glare made him fall a little more in love with her.

'What?' Kieran arched an eyebrow at his sister before closing the bedroom door on her and heading for the shower.

EIGHTEEN

Kieran jogged down the stairs to an eerily quiet house, he knew Lorna had wanted a run but began to hope she might have gone with the wolves if that's where they all were.

'There you are,' Lorna said as she emerged from the living room, seemingly having forgotten catching him with his jeans unbuttoned, 'Have you seen Kia?'

'Not since she left the living room last night.' Kieran shook his head. 'She's not picking up her phone?'

'No, she left it here.' Aiden appeared from the study, the look on his face thunderous.

'Why is it such an issue?' Kieran scowled.

'Because we can't have her sniffing around Cain, and she needs to ease off on hunting for my brother, it's not healthy how much time she's spending chasing ghosts.'

'Firstly, that's your brother. Secondly, how soon would you give up on chasing Lorna if she went missing?' Kieran's scowl stayed in place.

'If I knew she was dead?'

'If you *knew* she wasn't.'

'Kia thinks he's still alive. And believe me, having seen how either of them reacts to thinking the other is dead . . . I don't think whatever you're accusing her of is what's going on here.'

'If she goes after Cain by herself, I can't guarantee the safety of this pack.'

'And what if she's right and he is playing dirty? We're all dead anyway.' Kieran tried to reign in the frustration in his voice and realised he was failing.

Shooting a glance at Lorna, expecting her to stand up for Aiden, he found her stood with her arms folded, taking it all in.

Aiden followed his line of sight and whatever he saw in Lorna's stoicism calmed him slightly.

'We need to know what has happened to Nick. Kia believes he's being tortured. IF that is in some way related to either Cain or the Baxter issue I'm dealing with, we can't leave him for dead,' Lorna said calmly. 'It also means we're in bigger trouble than we thought.'

At a loss for words, Aiden huffed and walked back into the study.

Lorna inclined her head in the same direction and she and Kieran followed him to find Acheron and Saracen in there already.

'Back so soon?' Kieran nodded to Saracen.

'It was always my intention to stay last night, but circumstances being as they were, it was best to return to my pack. You don't turn down a full brunch buffet when Sookie has prepared it.'

Before he could ask what time they were allowed in the food hall, the front door opened and closed and Kia strolled into the entrance hall.

'Kia,' Aiden called, his voice still betraying his anger.

'Yes?' She appeared in the doorway, the look on her face telling them all she'd registered his tone.

'Where did you go?'

'I went to see if Asha needed anything.'

'Without your phone?'

'It's charging.' Kia shrugged.

'Did you go anywhere else?'

'Of course not.'

'Did you take any detours between HQ and here?'

'I took a longer route than usual, but I did not stop anywhere.' Kia's eyes were as challenging as Aiden's questions.

'Were you seen?'

'I didn't parade through the Goldstone Hotel if that's what you're asking.' Kia rolled her eyes.

'Just around it?' Lorna's eyes were amused, but given her position on the sofa, only Kieran could see that.

'I was just doing an energy sweep, I didn't approach, nor did I see any werewolves.' Kia shook her head. 'May I go and assist Sookie?'

'Sure,' Aiden sighed, but growled as he sat on the sofa next to Lorna.

'Proactive as always,' Saracen said with a smirk, raising a mug of coffee to his lips.

'We just can't have her doing a Nick during this,' Aiden said, exasperated.

'Doing a *Nick*?' Kia bit out from the doorway, having made it just a few steps before they'd spoken about her.

'Kia, it hasn't escaped the attention of many, including Cain, that you do as you damned well please these days. Cain looks to be perfectly willing to use that to his advantage. Nick was exactly the same, especially in the months leading up to his . . .'

'Death?' Kia's eyes blazed.

'Yes, death. He'd be home by now if he wasn't dead, Kia you know that, we know that. Cain clearly knows that, or he wouldn't have set the date he did.' Aiden got up to face her.

'He's not dead. And if Cain knows he is, perhaps you should be asking yourself how.'

'Because he was obliterated in a building belonging to Cain's pack brother! We have to let him go,' Aiden growled.

'I will not give up without a body,' Kia growled back.

'Don't growl at me.'

'Don't give up on your brother. Don't let that fleabag have it all his own way!'

'Kia, I'm warning you, learn some fucking control.' Aiden's voice deepened, dangerously.

'I'm perfectly in control, which is more than any of us can say for this situation. You have a mutt running rings around you.'

'Kia . . .'

'I know you're doing the best you can for the good of the pack, but that asshole has had it all his own way so far, and if he continues to have it all his own way, who knows what he'll do next! If my jurisdiction as head guardian will help surviving members of this pack, should the worst happen, then I'll fucking well use whatever I've got,' Kia looked at everyone in the room in turn. 'Saracen is prepared to do the same.'

'Saracen isn't meddling before the event.'

'Neither am I! I'm just trying to find Nick whilst looking for warning signs he might be about to unleash the hounds.'

'He hasn't threatened that.'

'Nor has he promised he won't.'

'You could really do with Nick's brain on this one,' Saracen pointed out calmly.

'If anyone could find the calm in this whole mess, he would have,' Acheron agreed, sadly.

'He would have,' Kia choked out, tears welling in her eyes as she turned, ready to leave. 'Nick and I are a team, cut me some fucking slack.'

'Kia, you will leave Cain's territory untouched, you will avoid any risk of confrontation, or I will be forced to temporarily ex-communicate you,' Aiden warned as she took a deep breath to compose herself and headed for the door again.

'Why make it temporary?' Kia shot back over her shoulder, 'If Nick is dead, as you are so convinced, then I'm no longer family . . . and, if I'm that much of a psycho, then maybe it's for the best.'

Successfully exiting the office, Kia slammed the door closed as she left.

Falling back into the seat next to Lorna, Aiden raked his hands through his hair.

'It doesn't matter what she does, she can't bring Nick back and she can't stop the challenge now it's been laid,' Aiden said to the twins questioning faces.

'She's Nick's mate for a reason. She clearly needs to feel like she's doing something to help,' Saracen pointed out from where he was filling one of Acheron's armchairs with his large frame. 'And if she was allowed to help, you know she'd have Cain's pack dealt with tomorrow.'

'Not legally,' Aiden groaned.

'Perfectly legally,' Lorna scoffed.

'You guys have rules too.' Aiden smirked as he reached for Lorna's hand as it rested on her lap between them.

'We do,' Kieran agreed, 'But Kia, I think you'll find, especially now . . . might just slide outside of those bindings too.'

'You think she falls under Angeling lore?' Acheron asked.

'In part, especially with the wings, sure,' Kieran offered.

'You know . . .' Saracen started, thoughtfully, 'Excommunicating her would work in your favour if that's the case.'

'I won't back out of this challenge through loopholes!' Aiden stood up again and began pacing.

'We're not asking you to.' Lorna stood with him and slid her arms around his shoulders.

'We're offering you the chance to stop what is almost certainly going to be an unfair fight.' Saracen drained his mug and reached for the pot on Acheron's desk beside him for a refill. 'You really think he plans to beat you in a fair fight, teeth to claw?'

'No, I'm not worried about that.'

'You think he's so sure of himself that he's working off pure ego?' Saracen raised both eyebrows as he lifted the coffee mug to his lips again.

'Of course not,' Aiden growled in frustration. 'In all honesty? I expect him to instruct his pack to attack us the moment the first swipe is thrown.'

'Distracting you and culling our numbers, even if he is defeated,' Lorna said gently. 'He'll run before he'll let you kill him. This fight is to your death, to the death of the Barnes line, not his. You think I can sit back and watch that happen?'

As silence fell on the group, Acheron poured himself a coffee to empty the pot, and drank the contents of his cup down in one go.

'Could we loan Kia to you, Saracen?' Acheron asked, putting the cup back down.

'My pack is bound by the rules too. She would be just as restricted.' Saracen waved off the suggestion. 'Not that I wouldn't happily borrow your fiercest member.' He grinned.

'I think it might be time to get some food.' Lorna decided to change the subject when her brother's stomach rumbled.

'Great idea.' Saracen jumped up and led the wolves out of the office.

Lorna hung back in a manner that told Kieran to wait a moment, so he didn't even stand until they were alone.

'What do you think?' she asked him quietly.

'I agree, it's going to be a bloodbath.' Kieran nodded. 'I also think that Kia untethered, could put a stop to all of it.'

'Nick?'

'Alive.'

'What makes you think so?'

'Kia could have died the other night. She didn't.'

Realisation, and something like relief, dawned in Lorna's eyes.

'She intends to live.'

NINETEEN

'Hey, Lorna, do you need Kieran today?' Kia appeared from the kitchen as breakfast was ending.

'I'm due in a meeting with Declan at one, so not today.' Lorna checked her watch.

'Can I borrow you?' Kia asked him directly.

'Sure.'

'Depends on what for.' Lorna raised her eyebrows as Aiden glanced over from where he was deep in conversation with Saracen.

'Lucious stuff.' Kia shrugged.

'Right.' Lorna rolled her eyes.

Leaving Aiden and Saracen to make whatever wolfish decisions they were going to make without the help of the guardians in the pack, all four on site prepared to leave after brunch.

'So where are we going?' Kieran asked Kia as he buckled in after climbing into the passenger seat of her car.

'I really do want to see if I can get an audience with Lucious.' Kia looked into his eyes for a reaction.

'Not impossible, if Nick could always get one, why shouldn't you?'

'Because I don't really know where to start.'

At that moment the back door opened and Lorna jumped in, moving into the middle seat to peer between the front two.

'What do you want?' Kieran twisted round to look at her.

'About earlier . . .' Lorna looked to Kia.

'Aiden has a point,' Kia sighed.

'He does, but I want you to do everything in your power to make sure that asshole doesn't play dirty.'

'They're going to do that either way, surely?' Kieran looked between them.

'Cain has proven he's way too provocative to be civil on the day, when it comes,' Kia agreed. 'But I can't play dirty in return. Aiden's right, I have to behave myself or he'll insist I'm removed from proceedings.'

'He can't do that.' Kieran scowled.

'He can request it, but as you're a non-wolf member . . .' Lorna started.

'Technically . . .'

'Morph doesn't count,' Lorna smirked. 'He can report the pack to the registry for not playing by the rules.'

'He'd have too much to lose by doing that, he can't attack if eyes are on the pack. Right?' Kieran asked.

'Aiden would be the one investigated, the pack name muddied,' Lorna offered.

'And Cain could slink back into his hole knowing we'd forever be watching our backs for the next attack. He doesn't need to kill Aiden to destroy all the family has built over the generations,' Kia pointed out.

'That's a point, wasn't this whole thing with Acheron in the first place?' Kieran's scowl deepened.

'It still is,' Kia's eyes slid his way. 'He throws Nick's name around a lot. Killing, or at least threatening Aiden, when Nick is already missing is hurting Acheron more than the pack. Don't even get me started on Sookie.'

'What about Sookie?' Lorna inched back in surprise.

'There's history between Cain and Sookie,' Kia admitted.

'In a pre-Acheron way?'

'In a they-fought-over-her way.' Kia's eyes widened.

'Great. So, what can we do if we're bound by certain rules too?' Kieran asked.

'Am I?' Kia looked at Lorna. 'Being no ordinary guardian?'

'You're certainly not,' Lorna replied with a smirk. 'See what Lucious says, if you find him.'

'Alright,' Kia answered simply, meeting Lorna's eyes as the back door opened again and Ashlie fought her way into the car, shoving Lorna over a bit as she clambered in.

'What's happening here? Guardian's mother's meeting without me??'

'We've got shit to do Ash, as have you.' Kia rolled her eyes at her friend.

'Looks like conspiracy to me.' Ashlie eyeballed them all in turn.

'Never!' Lorna smirked as she started moving for the opposite door. 'Right, I have places to be, fill me in later!'

And with that she was gone, leaving Ashlie glaring at Kia.

'Where are you two going?'

'Relax Ash, I'll give him back later.' Kia grinned.

'Fuck you,' Ashlie sniped, trying to hold back a smirk, 'I'll be at the shelter later, I'm on the evening shift.'

Lorna stuck her head back in the back door. 'See you all there, with pizza! Don't forget the garlic bread.'

'Can you even have garlic bread?' Kieran teased.

Lorna blinked in a manner that told him she hadn't thought about it.

'I fucking hope so!' she said finally and was gone again.

'How did she hear us?' Ashlie whispered, leaning between the front two seats.

'She heard me,' Kieran looked to his hair line to tell them she'd been in his head. 'It's somewhere we can check in away from here.'

'Gotcha.' Ashlie nodded. 'In which case, Kia, my usual?'

'Got it.' Kia smiled fondly over her shoulder. 'Aren't you leaving a bit early?'

'Unless you need me to eavesdrop on how the wolves think they're going to handle this situation, I think I'd best run some errands before my shift.'

'Such as?' Kieran asked, aware he was taking a little too much interest.

'Well, last I checked, beyond pack feasts, and pizza deliveries of mercy, a girl needs something in her cupboards.' Ashlie rolled her eyes. 'I'm a dried-out block of cheese away from starvation.'

'That does sound like disaster waiting to happen,' Kieran agreed.

'My turn to run then.' Ashlie gripped them both by the shoulder as she started sliding back across the seat, squeezing Kieran's as she shot him a look he found puzzling. It was a look that either said, "Thanks for everything" or "Until next time."

Kia watched her go, bandaged hand and all before looking to Kieran when the door was finally shut.

'She's not that clumsy.'

'Clumsy enough to fall back into my bed,' Kieran offered Kia a smile.

Kia grinned to herself as she started the engine. 'Perve.'

'Medic.' Kieran laughed watching Ashlie load her bag into her own car as they pulled away.

TWENTY

'So what's the plan?' Kieran asked as they sped away from the pack house.

'Head for the entrance to the Lucious's encampment in the Black Mountains and hope for the best.'

'You remember how to get there?'

'I've been more than once.' Kia shot him a look across the car. 'You don't?'

'My brain went fuzzy within a day, assumed that to be some kind of charm on the gates.'

'Must be another Nick thing.' Kia bit her lip.

'What are you going to ask him if you do see him? He's not exactly the most chatty being out there.' Kieran reached out to turn the radio on low.

'Hoping I won't need to ask anything, that he'll give me the words I need to hear, and I'll know what my next steps are.'

Even as she finished speaking, Kia's in-car phone system blared into life.

'Shit, I meant to get that disconnected again,' Kia hissed looking at the withheld number.

'It wouldn't be . . .'

'It would,' Kia accepted the call.

'Find him.'

That was it, two words, two syllables, in the commanding tone of the creature many of the city's monsters called the Dark Prince himself.

'I don't want to know how he did that.'

'Relax, he knew we were coming, that's all.' Kia sped up as she took the connecting road into the city rather than continuing around it.

'So now where?'

'How do you sneak around a hotel without arousing suspicion?'

'That hotel? You don't. Not right now.' Kieran shook his head.

'I want to tear it apart.' Kia's knuckles were white on the steering wheel, even as she slowed to join city traffic.

'You think they'd be stupid enough to take him there if they had him?'

'I think it's the one place they know we can't look,' Kia growled.

'But if we could prove he was there, would that help Aiden?'

'Probably.'

'How are werewolves with morphs?'

'What do you mean?'

'Does morphing also change your smell?'

Kia's head whipped round so fast, Kieran wasn't sure how she didn't get whiplash.

'Sort of.'

'Only sort of?'

'Yeah, my smell muddies in with it.' Kia's eyes searched the road as though the other vehicles would offer more ideas. 'Cain would still know me.'

'Alright, well, even as a morph then you're not going to just stroll in the door and take a look around. You'll need to get close to a member of staff. Let's think, where in a hotel would you stash a creature as big as Nick?' Kieran pushed.

'They wouldn't get him to the penthouse unseen.'

'Would they really care about that? Most of their guests are from beyond the city.'

'Everyone still knows who the current angeling is.'

'But they might not know he's missing.'

'It would look pretty suspect if he did anything other than walk in the doors himself.'

'OK so they'd take him in a staff entrance and maybe even a service elevator,' Kieran mused. 'So most of the staff are going to be in the pack's pocket, if not pack members themselves. The same as at Angelo's.'

'Could even be some staff crossover there.'

'If that's the case, what about the basement? It's bound to be full of service quarters, boiler rooms, laundry rooms. The hotel is massive, there could be a real warren of rooms beneath it. What do you think?'

'I'm thinking what if that basement happens to have an underground entrance?'

'It's bound to for fire safety purposes . . .' Kieran trailed off.

'OK, sounds like I'm going in.'

'I don't think I can come with you,' Kieran said, though he was hopeful she'd have a solution.

'Best you don't either way I think. I'll outlaw myself if I have to, if it gets us the proof we need. You won't be so lucky.'

'I was thinking more that I'm too easily spotted. Even with the guardian glamour tricks. I can't shapeshift the way you, or even Lorna, can.'

'Aww, you have talents all of your own.' Kia pouted playfully.

'And I like it that way, but it makes me even more conspicuous.'

Steering the car into the curb, Kia pulled over.

'Switch with me,' Kia said and jumped out of the car before he could argue.

Diving out and passing her as she rounded the nose of the vehicle, Kieran jumped in the driver's seat.

'Where to?'

'Drop me at the library,' Kia instructed as she fastened her seatbelt. 'I'm going to want a look at the floorplan of that building before I even think about going in, and the library is the safest place to access the plans.'

'If you're seen on camera?'

'I won't be doing anything else today as me,' Kia announced. 'Meet me at Shelter Two at eight.'

Once they reached the city library, Kia jumped out. Refusing to tell Kieran any more of her plans, she instantly blended into the crowd as her hair colour, height and clothing changed three times before he lost sight of her.

TWENTY-ONE

When Kieran made it to the shelter at eight, he found Ashlie already there by herself. He'd considered spending the afternoon with Lorna on the pretence of dragging her out of Vampire meetings, but she'd assured him those meetings were non-negotiable and refused to play.

With HQ off limits, he'd found himself at an unusually loose end. So he'd gone back to the apartment, changed, and hit the on-site gym instead.

Ashlie was sat at reception with her feet on the desk and her phone in hand.

Before Kieran had chance to open his mouth, or put the pizzas he was carrying down, Kia breezed in around him.

'OI! I could have been anyone!' Kia knocked Ashlie's feet from the desk.

Her chair hovered on two legs from a moment as she caught herself telekinetically before throwing the phone onto the desk and jumping up to stick her nose on the boxes of pizzas.

'I saw you coming. I know not just anyone can let themselves in here,' Ashlie replied but gazed up at Kieran. 'Which one of these is mine?'

'The top one I think.' Kieran held out the stack so she could retrieve it.

'Just in time. I'm starving. Thank you!' she gushed as she fell back into the desk chair to throw open the lid.

'Where's Lorna?' Kia asked, selecting her pizza from the pile and plopping herself down in one of the two reception armchairs.

'I'm here.' Lorna appeared through the front door. 'What did I miss?'

'Absolutely nothing,' Kieran deadpanned wishing that he'd had a chance to get a word in edgeways with Ashlie before Kia had waltzed in and likewise a chance to ask Kia how she'd got on before Lorna arrived.

He tossed her two of the three remaining boxes and setting his own down, wandered into the office in search of a spare chair. When he returned Lorna was lifting a chunk of garlic bread out of one of the boxes.

They all stopped to watch her for a moment.

'Will you all stop staring at me like I might combust?' Lorna paused.

'But you might,' Kieran reasoned.

Lorna shrugged and took a large bite as they all continued to watch her. Chewing thoughtfully for a moment, she pulled a face. No one spoke for a moment, then a self-satisfied grin spread across her face.

'Seems I'm all good!' she mumbled around a second mouthful. 'So how did everyone get on this afternoon?'

'Food shopping, all done,' Ashlie announced.

'Gym for me,' Kieran admitted.

'You were free this afternoon?' Ashlie asked quickly, forgetting herself.

'Unexpectedly, yes,' Kieran said slowly, a smile creeping over his face when he read what she was thinking all over her face.

'I needed to ditch him for what I had to do,' Kia said with a shrug.

'I don't suppose you had a vision to deal with Cain? Or managed to get a map to Nick from Lucious?' Lorna groused.

'Not quite.' Kia's eyes slid Lorna's way.

'But did you manage to get an audience with him?'

'Sort of.' Kieran nodded.

'His two words, down the phone, were "Find him",' Kia said.

'Which means there's something of him to find in the first place?' Lorna raised an eyebrow.

'Exactly. Now, where could he possibly be?'

'The one place we're not allowed to look?' Lorna kept the eyebrow in place. 'Tell me you didn't?'

'I didn't.'

'You didn't?' Kieran looked up from his own pizza.

'No. We were right, most of the staff are werewolves. I traced the underground fire escapes and tested morphing into an unsuspecting waitress to get near the staff entrances, but there were just too many of them milling around. If I'd started going anywhere that waitress didn't need to be it would have been obvious.'

'How many?' Lorna had stopped eating.

'A lot. Two or three on every entrance.'

'Which suggests he's expecting company,' Ashlie pointed out.

'Or desperately doesn't want any,' Kia offered a nod.

'But you and Nick are connected, how would they keep you off each other's radar if he's not dead?'

'I don't know,' Kia admitted sadly. 'But I suspect that's what my nightmares are all about.'

'And if he did pop up on radar, who would feel it?' Lorna asked.

'Provided he's not blocking people out deliberately, it would be myself, Lucious and perhaps Sookie, in that order. Why?'

'Not the dragons?'

'No, he always managed to keep them out. As helpful as that might have been though.' Kia picked at the crust of the latest slice of pizza. 'Asha would need to see someone who had seen him to know anything.'

'Funny how she was prevented from coming to the meeting yesterday,' Ashlie said in a casual tone, but when they all looked at her, her eyes said something else entirely.

'Shit.'

They all fell silent for a moment at Lorna's understatement.

Kieran was trying not to stare at Ashlie, finding himself more and more drawn to watching her and knowing it was dangerous to his health, when he saw Kia drop her pizza cheese-side down back into the box out of the corner of his eye.

By the time she came out of the vision, they were all watching her.

'Fuck,' she whispered and closed the lid on the last two slices of pizza.

'Where do you need to be?' Kieran asked, closing the lid on his own box.

'Somewhere I can't go.' Kia looked to them all in turn. 'The Goldstone Hotel.'

'Somewhere none of us can really go.' Lorna scowled. 'Why give you that vision?'

Kieran met Kia's eye with a pointed look.

'Can we go?' Ashlie asked Lorna but dragged her eyes to Kieran. 'We're new to the pack and not directly associated with any Barnes family members.'

'I don't think any of us should go,' Kia admitted. 'A werewolf just ripped a girl's throat out in a room on the thirty-second floor.' Kia raked her fingers through her hair.

'Who do we send in a situation like that?' Ashlie asked Lorna.

'Potentially no one. We don't get visions for werewolves, it's got to be a glitch.' Kieran folded his arms.

'The Fates don't do *glitches*.' Lorna glared at her brother. 'I know you've never agreed.'

'Then they do Lucious's bidding, and that's just as bad,' he pointed out.

'Have you got the wolf's name?' Lorna turned a frown on Kia.

'Not this time, just a surname. Brown.'

'That really narrows it down.' Ashlie dutifully jumped up from the computer to let Kia at it, but Kia waved her off. 'Perhaps it's the cue we need to report him?'

'Do you want to call it in with Aiden?' Kieran asked Lorna.

'I will, but we can't ignore it regardless.'

'Then we'll do it, and we'll go together,' Ashlie repeated her offer. 'Or I'll do it and Kieran can keep watch. I'll be in and out unseen before you, or they, know it. Even if they do see me, it's guardian business, so maybe let Mia know too?'

'I'll call the registry and Mia to officiate handover, that way it's logged as guardian business in all possible places,' Kia said as she dug her phone out of her pocket and placed the call in the hallway even as Ashlie was shrugging her jacket on.

'Will you both stay here until we get back?' Kieran asked his sister as he stood up.

'We'll cover this place but if either of us gets another vision we'll work it out. Let's hope it's a slow night.' Lorna raised both eyebrows and bit into the last chunk of her garlic bread.

TWENTY-TWO

After Kia passed the vision directly to Ashlie so she was in control of the execution and knew who she was looking for, Kieran and Ashlie had left for the hotel.

'I don't like this,' Ashlie said, shaking her head as they approached the hotel.

'What's to like?' Kieran agreed, his voice a low grumble of aggression.

'Spending more time with me?' Ashlie gasped, mock affronted.

'We spend most of our time together in a state of undress,' Kieran pointed out.

'I haven't heard you complaining.' Ashlie shrugged before strutting straight through the main doors and into the lobby.

'What if I wanted to spend more time with you with our clothes on?' Kieran asked as they called the elevator.

'You know I don't date,' Ashlie replied. 'Besides, that's what pack dinners are for.'

'For now,' Kieran said under his breath.

Ashlie met his eyes sadly.

'Well, if we survive February, ask me again.'

'Deal.' Kieran smirked as they boarded the elevator.

'This hotel is a bit quiet, don't you think?' Ashlie's eyes scanned the lobby as the doors closed on them.

Only two members of staff manned reception and barely three residents existed in the lobby. Two sat on a sofa with coffees and newspapers, another wheeling a suitcase out of the building.

'It is the dead of winter.' Kieran's lips twitched in amusement.

'How do you afford to run a forty-storey hotel without guests?' Ashlie asked as she scanned the elevator for security cameras.

'Maybe there are apartments in the block too?' Kieran rolled his eyes. 'Most hotels have permanent residents.'

'This one must have a fair few.' Ashlie turned to him and gripped his arm, showing him exactly what she was thinking.

Realisation dawned in Kieran's eyes and he felt a ball of dread settle in the pit of his stomach as he stared into her jade eyes.

Gripping her hand so that she couldn't break contact, Kieran used her touch as a way into her head.

'We should leave.'

'We can't. We have a job to do.'

'It could be a trap.'

'Then let's hope it was set for Kia and we've thrown them for a loop.'

When the elevator reached floor thirty-two, the guardians moved swiftly towards room fifteen.

The hotel was eerily silent, in a manner that seemed unnatural. Either there were no other residents on floor thirty-two, or the whole place was soundproofed. Kieran felt as though his ears had been stuffed with cotton wool as their footsteps fell on thick, spongey carpet.

At room fifteen they made eye contact, ready to break the door down and catch the offender by surprise.

Only the door was already ajar.

Ashlie looked to Kieran, who met her eyes and looked back down the corridor.

If there had been a struggle, or a screaming match, no one had come to see what the problem was, and seemingly staff hadn't yet been alerted to the mess inside the room.

Kieran eased the door open further and Ashlie crept in ahead of him.

The smell of blood wafted into the hallway as Kieran stayed near the door in case anyone approached the room.

'Well, that's problematic.'

'What?' Kieran looked back.

'He's already dead.'

'What?' Kieran repeated.

'Come and see for yourself,' Ashlie hissed.

Glancing back at the door as though he expected it to lock shut behind him, Kieran reluctantly moved past the bathroom to take a peek at the bed where there were indeed two bodies.

Though one was far more recently dead than the other.

Blood was still oozing from the gaping hole in the wolf's throat.

'Think they killed him when they saw us coming?' Ashlie placed her hands on her hips.

'As I believe you're aware. We deal with our own.'

Kieran stepped in front of Ashlie has Cain appeared in the doorway.

'We're here under orders.' Ashlie stepped around Kieran as he kept his focus on Cain, blocking their exit.

'Pack orders?' Cain's eyes flashed.

'No, vision orders. You can check with the registry and guardian council member, Mia Sanderson,' Ashlie continued.

It took everything Kieran had not to drag his eyes to Ashlie at that point, like her best friend, she was certainly a firecracker when it came to holding her own.

'If this wolf isn't a pack member, we can arrange for cleanup to remove the body for you,' Ashlie suggested.

'He's certainly not one of mine,' Cain laid on the charm, 'but of course, I couldn't have bloodshed in my hotel either.'

'It is unusual that a guardian should be dispatched to deal with a werewolf in the first place,' Kieran said evenly.

'Probably because he was a lone wolf. I can provide the registry with his check-in details if it pleases you?' Cain smiled.

'Cleanup will get them off you either directly or through reception, so they can file him correctly with the registry,' Ashlie explained even as she fired off a message to the on-duty team. 'They'll be around twenty minutes. Do you have any idea who his victim was?'

'Prostitute, probably.' Cain's eyes slid to her phone and he stood straight. 'Now if you'll excuse me, I have a hotel to run. Please inform housekeeping when the room is ready for them.'

Kieran held his breath as Cain made his exit, wondering where the catch was.

'Let's see if she has any ID.' Ashlie sighed and began tip toeing around the blood-splattered room.

'Hard to know what's his blood and what's hers at this point.' Kieran gazed at the sheer amount of blood on the ceiling. 'Careful, some of it is still dripping.'

Ashlie blew a disappointed breath through her lips. Dealing with murder scenes was nothing new. The senselessness of it never failed to sucker punch her though.

They used the time waiting for cleanup to hunt down the girl's ID, though both wished they hadn't.

Their fellow guardian was barely eighteen.

'Do you suppose she was working?'

'I hope not.' Kieran surveyed the room again. 'Let's hope it was classic wrong place wrong time.'

As soon as cleanup arrived, they relayed what they knew and made a hasty retreat, informing reception that the head of the team would let them know when they were done so the time they left would be on record.

'Can I ask why you don't date?' Kieran asked as they headed back towards the shelter.

'You may not.' Ashlie kept her focus forwards. 'But if I ever change my mind, you'll be one of the first to know.'

'You have a ranking? Good to know.'

'No.' Ashlie shook her head but still wouldn't look at him. 'I'd have to inform Kia first, then I suspect I'd need to ask your sister's permission.'

He wasn't sure whether she was joking with him or not, it was hard to get a read on her, which he could tell was just as deliberate.

'Obviously,' he agreed, hoping to lighten the tone.

They walked back to the subway in silence, it wasn't until they were on a train that Ashlie spoke again.

'There was something about all of that that just seems really . . . off.'

'It certainly wasn't a normal vision.' Kieran agreed. 'What are you thinking?'

'I don't know, I just can't see the point in it. I mean if Lucious wanted Kia in that building, and they seemed to want Kia in that building . . . it's not going to be for the same reasons, is it?'

'Unlikely,' Kieran agreed. 'But that would suggest Kia is fated to enter that building at some point.'

'Fuck, I hope not.' Ashlie's eyes narrowed to slits.

'We've got her back.'

'You see her doing any dumb shit and you can't stop her, call me.' Ashlie finally looked at him.

'Alright.'

TWENTY-THREE

Kieran was woken by the sound of a commotion in the pack house. His body instantly went into an all-too-familiar overdrive, and he jumped out of bed and into a pair of jeans before taking a deep breath to shake off the angst that had sat on his chest since his teenage years and move for the door at a more casual pace.

Ruckus in the house didn't mean your family was being attacked, didn't mean you and your parents were in danger.

Not anymore.

Though he realised as he opened the door, being part of a pack, especially this pack, had put the twins right back in a position to tear those wounds apart.

He looked to Lorna's bedroom door opposite, having known all along that was one of the reasons she'd given him that room.

The door was open and the room was clearly empty, so he headed for the source of the noise.

He wondered how many people were in the house to hear the commotion, given that the wolves came and went as they pleased.

When he'd got back to the shelter with Ashlie, they'd found Lorna by herself. Kia had been called off on another vision, but his sister had reassured them that it was just a vampire, nothing pack related, so she'd let her go.

Deciding to wait for her to return, the twins had kept Ashlie company. Given the frosty reception Lorna had given Ashlie in the morning, he was pleased to see his sister was on her best behaviour, though Ashlie seemed glad of the distraction when one of the residents needed her to go upstairs and replace a lightbulb in one of the bathrooms.

Once she returned the trio had picked at cold leftover pizza until Kia strolled back through the door promising that everything had gone to plan, even offering them a twirl to prove the clothes she'd left in weren't blood splattered.

'Ah good, you're up.' Aiden appeared at the top of the stairs appraising Kieran before he hammered on Kia's door.

'What the hell, Aiden?' Kia opened the door in her nightwear, rubbing her eyes at the urgency.

Kieran took in the difference in demeanour in Kia than himself. Like Nick, she didn't fly into panic mode unless the zip of threat was in the air. He took that as a cue to relax his shoulders, until he saw the thunderous look on Aiden's face.

'Can I see you both in the office, please?' Aiden growled.

'Sure, give me a sec.' Kia shut the door.

Kieran considered waiting for her, but when he turned to speak to Aiden, he found him already halfway down the stairs.

Glancing over the banister into the large entrance way below, Kieran found several pack members stood around looking shell-shocked.

Following Aiden to the office doorway, he realised Kia was at his back by the time he made it to the ground floor having thrown on some jeans and a t-shirt.

'What's happened?' Kia asked as Aiden ushered them both inside the office.

'Just go in and take a seat,' Aiden's voice was quiet, but he wouldn't look at her.

Kia ducked inside when Kieran motioned for her to go first.

Finding Lorna already seated inside, he raised both eyebrows questioningly, but she was looking at Kia too.

'What's happened?' Kia repeated, watching Aiden and realising he was giving a plastic box in the centre of the room a very wide berth. 'Who's in the box?'

'We believe it's Seth,' Acheron said gently.

'What? No.' Kia's voice was barely a whisper as she shook her head and peered into the box.

Sucking in a deep breath, she covered her mouth with her hands. What was in the tub was indescribable. Body parts of all sizes hacked to pieces and partially dissolved swam in the container in front of them.

'He's the only pack member unaccounted for,' Aiden confirmed.

Kieran tried to catch Kia's eye, but she was still staring hard at the box. He wasn't the *only* member unaccounted for.

'Obviously they didn't leave ID but then, I doubt you got the name of the wolf you slaughtered last night either?' Aiden continued, bearing down on Kia to take her gaze away from the box.

'I didn't kill a wolf last night.' Kia's head snapped up so fast, Kieran wondered if she got whiplash.

'Cain is claiming otherwise.' Aiden swiped a piece of paper from his father's desk. 'They want you gone. You disobeyed a direct order, and the code of conduct Pool Valley packs adhere to.'

'The only wolf any of us went near last night was the one I had a vision to kill.' Kia inched forward, making Aiden back up a step before he could stumble into the box. 'And because it was a wolf on Cain's grounds I didn't go. I sent Ashlie and Kieran in my place.'

'We called it in, and we were seen coming and going, we even spoke with Cain and cleanup,' Kieran confirmed.

'Did you have any other visions last night?' Aiden asked Kia, ignoring Kieran.

'I had a vampire kill.'

'Anything unusual about that kill?'

'A wolf attacked me on my way back to the shelter.'

It was Kieran's turn to gawp at Kia, she hadn't told any of them that.

'And what did you do?'

'I broke its neck,' Kia admitted after a moment.

'Any witnesses?'

'No, but I was careful not to make a mess, and I'm sure there was security footage outside the cinema it happened near. I could hack . . .'

'Does this look like a broken neck to you?!' Aiden grabbed something else off his father's desk and shoved it in Kia's face.

The front steps of the cinema had been given a red re-spray. The head of a werewolf hanging from a light fixture above the ticket booth.

'Obviously not, but that is the wolf and the cinema I told you about.'

'Can you prove this wasn't you?'

'If there's CCTV, yes.'

'If there isn't?' Kieran asked Aiden for her and got a glare for the trouble.

'I'll get to you in a moment. Cleanup told Lorna the room you visited was in a hell of a mess also.'

'Yes, it was. Cain told us he'd killed the wolf himself as it was wolf business, despite swearing the deceased was not one of his.'

'Aiden, Cain cannot possibly prove I did this.' Kia waved the photo back at him, having snatched it out of his hands.

'You cannot prove you didn't.'

'I can . . .'

'Kia, that cinema does not have security cameras. We already checked,' Acheron muttered.

'I don't kill for fun. And I don't put my family in danger for shits and giggles!' Kia tried not to laugh in outrage as she spoke.

'I can't account for your exact whereabouts after you left the shelter,' Lorna said, unnecessarily in Kieran's view.

'Given your reputation, you can understand how this looks, right?' Aiden placed his hands on his hips.

'I know how Cain wants it to look. So now what?' Kia balled her hands into fists to prevent from shaking as her voice deepened.

'I'm sending you to Saracen, he offered to keep you out of the way should something like this occur,' Aiden bit out.

'You can't do that!' Kia shouted. 'Banish me, send me back to the apartment. You can't just give me to another pack for safeguarding! That's degrading.'

'Where else would you go where someone can keep an eye on you?'

'Where my movements are tracked?! Are you fucking serious?'

'You can stay on site at guardian HQ, where you could continue working undisturbed,' Kieran offered.

Kia flinched.

'Mia would let you stay with them too,' Lorna chipped in making Kia bow her head in dismay.

'You basically want me chained, or muzzled, just as Cain demanded,' Kia forced through gritted teeth.

'Kia . . .' Aiden sighed, trying to retain grip on his anger. 'If we don't prove to them that we're keeping you at arm's length, he will kill someone else.'

'So he's already broken his own precious rules! You can't keep letting him do this to you Aiden! It's getting pathetic,' Kia bit out.

'And you can't keep answering me back. If you don't control yourself, I will banish you.'

'Don't bother. I'm leaving,' Kia yelled. 'I will not be leashed.'

'Fine, get out!' Aiden returned.

'I'm not going to Saracen,' Kia warned as she marched to the office door and threw it open. 'I will not lose my family *and* my freedom.'

'Then go, enjoy your freedom. But if someone else dies, don't ever come back,' Aiden growled out in a low, dangerous tone.

Kieran watched Kia leave the room without looking back and heard her run up the stairs to Nick's room.

'Was that totally necessary?!' Kieran turned on Aiden.

'Don't you start. Cain isn't impressed to have had non-wolf pack members on his property as it is.'

'We. Were. Working,' Kieran said slowly.

'I could have told you he'd kill the wolf if he discovered it.'

'But you didn't,' Kieran returned, 'and I doubt there is any protocol for what's actually happening here.'

'And what is that?' Aiden lifted his chin.

'You have a head guardian in your pack. Hell, you probably have more guardians on-site than any other pack on the planet. It's unprecedented, that's all.' Kieran shrugged.

'Cain has already stated his distaste for non-wolf pack members. We can't be sure that wasn't why Asha and Luca were attacked,' Lorna pointed out. 'Sending Kia away might have advantages, but . . .'

Lorna paused when Aiden's glare turned on her.

'But,' she continued, 'I think those of us who aren't werewolves should watch our backs a little more carefully.'

'You are werewolf,' Aiden snorted.

'Not fully, not even by half.' Lorna arched an eyebrow.

Kieran took in the exchange between Lorna and Aiden and decided it might be best not to know what they were up to. Instead, he let his gaze travel Acheron's way to see what he was making of it.

'Tell Kia the apartment is hers. Whatever happens,' Acheron said when he met Kieran's eye.

'Is that an indirect order to go after her?' Kieran queried as Kia reappeared in the hallway, two duffle bags slung over her shoulders as she left the house without another word to anyone.

There was silence as they waited for the skid of gravel as she drove away.

When the silence continued, Kieran nodded.

'Right.'

Heading back upstairs, he showered, changed and grabbed his keys.

When he returned to the hallway, Lorna was stood waiting for him.

'I don't want to know,' he said before she could open her mouth. 'But please offer my condolences to Dante if that bucket of slop does turn out to be Seth.'

'Being callous is my skill, not yours.' Lorna scowled in return.

'Just be certain before you take this any further.' Kieran softened slightly at the concern on her face. 'I don't care if Aiden is now playing his own games. You just tell me where and when you need me.'

'Right now, that's at HQ, Mia confirmed Kia has gone there.'

'With her bags?'

'I don't know, she might be visiting Luca.' Lorna offered a shrug and tossed him a paper bag. 'Grabbed you a croissant.'

Kieran caught it and tossed it back. 'Thanks, but no way of eating it on the bike, and besides, I'm suddenly not that hungry.'

'More for me then.' She nodded.

TWENTY-FOUR

'Some vacation you're having,' Mia peered over the top of her computer at Kieran as he let himself into her office.

'I've been working on my tan, can't you tell?' Kieran smirked. 'Where is she?'

'She's with Asha on the residential floor. They've been staying here.'

'I know. Has Kia requested a room?'

'Not that I know of. Why?' Mia glanced at Ben, who was typing furiously at his own desk.

He glanced up long enough to shake his head.

'With everything going on, it might be safer for various pack members to relocate in the coming weeks,' Kieran lied.

'We have room,' Mia offered.

'I know.' Kieran nodded. 'Thank you.'

The couple lived in an apartment on the top floor of the building, it was closer to work than Kieran would have preferred, but given they'd commissioned the building and had a say in designing it, it had made sense at the time and they'd just never left.

'You should make more use of our place,' Ben suddenly said without looking up. 'We leave a room ready for you or Lorna in case you ever need it. Got to be better than catching a few Z's in the doctor's quarters.'

'I'll bear that in mind.' Kieran offered a smile, knowing they were right, if they were working, he'd have their place to himself.

In fact, turning his phone off and spending a day up there was sounding like more of a vacation than he was getting.

'Still got a key?' Mia was smiling, thrilled at the idea that he might actually take them up on it.

'Of course.'

Which wasn't a lie, as aloof as he could be with his adoptive grandparents, Kieran wasn't immune to the draws of family time. Even if historically, that had only been when it suited him.

Leaving them to their work, Kieran wandered up to the residential floor which offered studio rooms, dorm rooms, a shared kitchen and at least four self-contained two-bedroom apartments for guardians who needed to go into emergency accommodation with their families.

Thankfully, that was rare, even in their line of work. But it was in one of those apartments that he found Asha, Luca and Kia.

'Hey, how are you?' Kieran asked Luca as he followed him inside.

'Gutted I don't heal as fast as a werewolf, or vampire, but I'm getting there.' He offered a pained chuckle and led Kieran to the small open-plan kitchen and living space where Kia and Asha were cradling hot drinks on one of two sofas. 'Hot chocolate?'

'Sure, thanks, but I can get it.'

'Hey, I'm not as broken as I was, I can grab it.' Luca waved Kieran away with one plaster-casted arm.

'He's not just being modest, he is healing well,' Asha promised Kieran when he took a seat.

'What did you get in injury bingo then?' Kieran asked brightly when Luca came back to the and handed him a drink.

'Three broken ribs, a cracked eye-socket, broken wrist, dislocated shoulder, and this baby here,' he pointed to an angry welt just into his hair-line, 'bled enough to freak Asha out and give me concussion.'

'Full house!' Kieran met the fist-bump Luca offered.

'It wasn't funny.' Asha glared at the pair of them.

'Come on, Kieran couldn't be a medic without a dark sense of humour. That's day one stuff, right?' Luca asked him.

'Oh yeah, they do a whole module on that shit,' Kieran agreed.

'Speaking of shit.' Kia eyeballed Kieran. 'Cut the crap and tell me why you're really here.'

'To see if everyone is OK.' Kieran met her stare. 'Not just you. Are you planning to stay here?'

'Where else would I go?' Kia bit back. 'I'm not going to sit around at the O'Neill's waiting for my ex-pack to be slaughtered. It's not like my duties here would suddenly cease.'

'Acheron says the apartment is yours. Whatever happens.'

'I can buy my own damned apartment,' Kia hissed.

'Those were his words. You don't have to do anything right now.'

Kia's resolve faltered as she considered the implications of leaving Nick's apartment and her gaze fell to the floor.

'You know this whole thing is a setup, right? What Cain's doing, what Aiden's done?' Kia groused quietly.

Kieran nodded, he knew, they all knew everyone had their own agenda, but he had to admit, he was starting to struggle to keep up.

'So, what are you going to do about it?' Asha asked Kia for Kieran.

'I can't go down there, they've made that abundantly clear. But at the same time I need to.' Kia sat back and folded her arms. 'To start with, I'll do what I can electronically.'

'Weren't you already doing that?' Luca asked, surprised.

'I've been trying to track individual wolves, I haven't been digging into the hotel itself.' Kia shrugged. 'That will help me keep my head down at least.'

'Just keep passing on any visions that take you anywhere near there to me,' Kieran said.

'You and I both know there's only two reasons I'd continue to get visions around that place,' Kia returned.

'Lucious wants you there, or Cain wants you there, we'd already agreed that.'

'Three then.'

'Three?'

'How is Lorna doing with the vampire situation? Wasn't there something about some bloodletting still going on? In guardians?'

'What would Cain be doing getting involved with vampires?'

'I don't know,' Kia admitted. 'But bloodsuckers haven't been totally absent in all this.'

Kieran thought back to the incident in the park with Ashlie.

'We're still getting visions as normal.'

'That's the only thing I can't get my head around either.'

'We got nothing either.' Luca sat back, setting one ankle on the opposite knee and attempting to cross his arms over his chest despite the cast.

'I'm certainly not going to ask you to try either.' Kia gave them both a pointed look, which was more of a warning, as she pulled her phone from her pocket.

Kieran watched her thumb open a message and jump up.

'Cain's in the bar.'

'What?!' He also got to his feet.

'That's bad, right?' Luca narrowed his eyes.

'It won't be good.' Asha rolled her eyes at him.

'I'll come with you.' Kieran fell in step with Kia as she had already started moving.

'I've got to see this . . .' Luca also stood.

'No, you don't,' Asha sang, 'You're going to show me how to do the odd jobs you're insisting on finishing for Mia despite being on sick leave.'

'I don't think either of us can fix the rope net in the training arena,' Luca groused.

'I'll be back to help with that.' Kieran looked over his shoulder as he followed Kia out of the apartment.

'One corner is fully hanging off, it's been dangling for weeks,' Kia muttered as they walked.

'Oh, that. I've fixed it before.' Kieran shrugged.

'Well, you did a shit job.'

'Not if it's lasted the five years since I last did it.' He grinned.

When they entered the bar, Mia was holding fort in some vague attempt to hold professionalism. But Kieran could see she had said very little to the wolves milling around the street entrance.

'Hasn't it been made clear enough to you that due to the circumstances, this is highly inappropriate?' Kieran opened his mouth before Kia had a chance.

Not that it mattered, Cain ignored Kieran completely as Kia took an extra step forward, her arms folded.

'You should have been told to leave for Emerald Acres.'

'No one tells me where to go,' Kia replied. 'Least of all you.'

'Aiden promised me he'd send you away.'

'You and I both know there was no justification for that.'

'Did he not show you our proof?'

'He showed us an unidentified pool of body parts, if we're talking proof,' Kia drawled. 'Think before you speak, Cain, you're on my turf now, no one here is as willing to hear your shit as Aiden is. You have no standing in this building, you cannot frame me for your crimes in here.'

She kept her arms folded as she spoke, unwilling to offer the so-called alpha even a hair's breadth of an inch.

'The council might have a different opinion.' Cain glanced at Mia, but there was nothing but disdain in his eyes.

'All creatures are welcome here to drink, but if you came here to see me, it was a wasted trip. We have no business here.' Kia drew his attention back to her.

'It's pack business.'

'I have no pack. Not anymore. But I am head guardian,' Kia said evenly. 'So if you want to make this personal, fleabag, you need to remember that on this platform, I outrank you.'

Cain finally seemed to see the rest of the room around him, and how many eyes were on him. Kieran followed his gaze around the room while Kia remained focused. Many of the guardians in the room were looking Cain up and down as though they were all planning exactly what to do with him should a vision hit.

Regardless, a slow grin began to spread across Cain's face.

'Do they know your past?'

'Silly puppy.' Kia pouted, drawing Cain's eyes back to her fast enough to give his optic nerves whiplash. 'We're a building full of legalised murderers, there isn't a guardian in the bar who wouldn't grant you a very slow and very messy death if a vision showed them exactly what *you* are capable of.'

'You give me a call when you get that vision,' Cain hushed as he leant forward, causing Kieran's eyes to narrow.

'I'll give you a call when I find proof you're manipulating the system,' Kia returned. 'Now, sit.'

Cain started to laugh, but his chuckling soon turned to a grunt of pain as Kia commanded his body to buckle and shrink into a sitting position. Sean lurched forward, but Kia's attention was already on him.

'You, play dead.'

As Sean fell to the floor in a dead faint, the rest of the wolves took a step back.

'The next command will be roll over, any volunteers?' Kia asked. 'No? Good. Now get out.'

As soon as her hold was released Cain jumped up and put himself in her face, Kia again remained still, she'd already proven she didn't need to move to hurt him, just as Lorna had promised.

'I'll be reporting this to Aiden.'

'He's no longer my alpha, and I'm no longer his concern. You can't even report this to the council because, need I remind you, you're on *my* turf.'

'I knew you were dangerous.'

'Stop showboating, everyone in this room knows I'm dangerous. It comes with the job.'

'Reckless then.'

'If you're not out that door in three seconds I'll show you reckless and solve Aiden's problem.' Kia's whole shield fizzed with electricity in warning.

With a growl, Cain turned and walked out, leaving the rest of the wolves he'd brought with him, including a dazed Sean, to hurry after him.

'Stupid bastard,' Kia hissed, turning to find Mia behind her with a drink.

'Should have zapped him while you had him on trespassing.' Mia winked as Kia downed the shot of rum.

'Just wait until you see what I'm actually going to do to him when I get the chance,' Kia bit out.

'You can't really do anything,' Kieran reminded her.

'Under the right circumstances, there's plenty. I just didn't want to redecorate the bar today.'

TWENTY-FIVE

Kieran was in the process of beating the crap out of the punchbag in the gym at HQ when Kia burst through the door.

They'd spent the rest of the day taking direction from Luca regarding the odd jobs he'd fallen behind with. It hadn't been enough for Kieran who had felt low-level on edge since being woken up that morning, so he'd taken to the gym. Though, glancing at the clock as he removed his earbuds, he realised he'd only been in there fifteen minutes.

'Decided to do a rage workout?' Kieran took in the thunderous look on her face as he caught the bag and steadied it.

'Yes, but not here. I have to run.'

'Run? Where?' Kieran's eyes slid to the handful of guardians having a chat over by the weights and lowered his voice.

'I've had a call from a Oakley. It's not good.'

'Not another body?'

'No, but could be. Ramsey has also gone missing.'

'Fuck.'

'Yeah, and it turns out Seth had been missing several hours, but no one had noticed. Oakley said Aiden's plan is to get them all to buddy up from now on.'

'This can't continue.'

'I'm not going to let it.' Kia nodded her agreement. 'Cover for me.'

'You're on a vision,' Kieran stated. 'Do you need backup?'

'No. It's best no one knows what I'm about to do.'

'That sounds ominous.'

'It could be,' Kia replied evenly.

'Kia . . .'

'Keep an eye on my family. And my best friend,' Kia said quietly, meeting his eyes.

'I will,' Kieran muttered back. 'If you need me. . .'

'I'll call.'

Giving herself barely the time for a single nod, Kia left the facility.

Replacing his earbuds, he didn't hear the music he had been listening to, instead, he found his phone ringing. Connecting the call without thinking he answered quickly.

'Hello?'

'Kieran,' a panicked voice hushed down the line.

'Ashlie?'

'Yeah, I got your number off Kia, I hope you don't mind.'

'Not at all,' Kieran almost smiled, but her tone was too urgent. 'What's the matter?'

'I think I'm being followed.'

'What?' Kieran felt his heart kick into overdrive even as his feet began moving towards the locker room. 'Where are you?'

'I've ducked into a convenience store two blocks from HQ, I was on my way there to use the gym.'

'Really this time?'

'This is no time to joke Kieran, do you know how much actual gym memberships cost?'

'OK, OK, it's just, that's where I am. I'll come and meet you. Pretend like you're buying protein bars or something.'

'Gross. But OK,' Ashlie scoffed. 'I'll message you the store.'

'I know the one, it's alright.'

Foregoing his locker, Kieran pocketed his phone and ran from the building.

The store really wasn't that far away, he made it there in two minutes.

Slowing to a stroll as he entered the shop, he scanned the aisles quickly. He found Ashlie paying too much attention to the snack section and watched out of the corner of his eye as a couple who had been milling by the magazines at the opposite end near the registers nudged each other and left the shop.

He swallowed down the lump of granite that hit him in the chest to know she was right, and offered a quiet cough to get her attention.

'Hey!' She threw her arms around his neck, catching him off-guard despite how excited-friend she tried to make it look.

'Are you alright?'

'Shaken, especially as Kia told me what's happened today.'

'Did she tell you Ramsey is missing?'

'Yeah, I called her first.'

'Right.' Kieran nodded, trying to stop himself from pulling a face at being second choice.

'Ready to hit the gym then?' Ashlie began walking in the direction of the exit.

'Sure.' Kieran followed closely behind, keeping an eye out for the couple of stalkers. In his haste he hadn't taken a close enough look for tell-tale signs of species, but if he'd had to put money on it, he'd have said they were wolves. 'Lead the way.'

Two hours later Kieran ran his fingers through his hair, letting it fall over his face and back onto his shoulders as he contemplated the shot of whiskey on the bar in front of him. It had been a long day.

He'd humoured Ashlie when she'd suggested they do some circuit training, and followed her around the gym for ninety minutes before they'd agreed it was time to hit the showers.

He didn't know where she'd gone after that, she hadn't said goodbye, but equally she hadn't been around when he left the locker room.

Asha was back behind the pumps, admitting that it was easier to put in shifts and keep herself busy. Especially when she was living just a few floors away.

He had no idea Ashlie was sat at a table behind him, though he should have felt her eyes drinking in the way his black t-shirt was clinging to the muscles of his back and shoulders.

'You should go to bed.'

He looked up to see Asha in front of him, drying a glass.

'You both should.'

'Both?' Kieran scowled as he fought a yawn and toyed with the glass.

When he looked up, Asha nodded to the booth over his shoulder.

Nonchalantly, he took up the glass, finished the last mouthful and glanced over his shoulder to finally see Ashlie, suddenly staring into a mug of one of Asha's finely crafted coffees.

'If she's waiting for Kia, we both know she'll have a long wait,' Asha cooed.

Kieran deliberately didn't turn back to the dragon at the bar, knowing she'd read him like a book. Instead, he slid off the bar, scooping up his leather jacket and heading over to the booth.

Ashlie stood as he approached but seemed to fall over her own feet and pitch hazardously towards the floor.

'Woah,' Kieran said as he caught her. 'Are you OK?'

'Sorry, yeah, I'm ridiculously clumsy when I'm tired.' She shook herself off as she straightened, but looked back to her half-drunk coffee.

'Finish your coffee, in fact, I'll join you, wait there.' Kieran turned to head back to the bar, but Asha was behind him, handing him a freshly made cappuccino. 'Thanks Asha,' he breathed, grateful.

'I'm not waiting for Kia,' Ashlie groused when Kieran nudged her back into the booth so he could join her.

'Do you want me to walk you home?' Kieran asked casually but caught the look of relief flash through her eyes.

'I don't need someone to walk me home.' Ashlie attempted to laugh at him. 'But . . .'

'But pack members are going missing, strong ones, and they're turning up in pieces,' Kieran finished for her. 'Strength in numbers is OK sometimes.'

'You just want to take me home to bed.' Ashlie smirked even as she nodded.

'I'm not gonna lie, as much fun as I'm sure that would be, sleep is my whole intention.'

'The coffee might say otherwise.' Ashlie smiled.

'This will get me home, that's enough.'

'That bad, huh?'

'It's just catching up with me I think.' Kieran rubbed his eyes before reaching for his cup.

'Comes in waves,' Ashlie agreed.

When she nodded, he was surprised she didn't pass out into the dregs of her drink there and then. Attempting to catch up with her, he took several mouthfuls of his own coffee while it was still too hot. Once she finished, he decided to abandon the remains of his.

'Alright, enough of that. Let's get out of here. I'll go get the bike out of the garage.'

'I don't think that's a great idea.' Ashlie wrinkled her nose. 'Clumsy when tired, remember.'

'Right. OK, we'll work something out.'

Putting his coffee down, Kieran got to his feet again and they left the bar, waving goodnight to Asha as they left.

'Can we walk to your place?' Kieran looked to Ashlie as they headed up the street in the direction of the store he'd rescued her from.

'Not really, I subwayed before going into the store.'

'When did you pick up the tail?'

'Walking from the subway I think.'

'Let's hope so or . . .'

'Or they know where I live.' Ashlie paled in the streetlights.

'I'll hail a cab when we reach the avenue,' Kieran mused, 'Perhaps we should move in together until this whole thing blows over.'

'Well, that's a way to get around my no-date rule,' Ashlie spluttered around a laugh.

'I'm serious, pack members have already been told to buddy up. I can take the sofa or something, either at Kia's or yours?'

Ashlie mulled his words over for the remainder of the block. When they reached the corner he started trying to hail a cab as she nodded.

'Perhaps I should pack a bag for Kia's,' she said. 'That way we're a triple buddy with Kia.'

'Sounds like a good idea,' Kieran agreed as a cab pulled up.

When the cab stopped outside a mock-townhouse across the city, Kieran settled the fare while Ashlie searched her gym bag for her keys.

In the time it took them to get out of opposite ends of the car, something broke out of the shadows and charged Ashlie, knocking her to the ground.

Slamming the car door shut, Kieran threw himself at the figure as it collected itself and turned ready to make a grab for Ashlie while she was down.

With a yell of pain from Ashlie, and a roar of frustration from the figure, all three tumbled into the gutter as the cab sped away, not wanting to be any part of what was happening.

Rolling, both guardians refocused fast and threw fireballs at the assailant, which on realising Ashlie wasn't alone, scrambled up and made a run for it.

'Fuck,' Kieran breathed, hearing the panic in his own voice as he sat up and reached for Ashlie. 'Are you OK?'

'Yeah, smacked my shoulder on something when I went down, but I'm alright,' she huffed. 'I think perhaps something's got it in for me tonight.'

Kieran didn't want to entertain that thought any more than he wanted to be sitting in the gutter in the dark. But he nodded and steered them both towards the front door of the townhouse.

It was a puzzle of apartments inside, with Ashlie stating that she was on the first floor. They walked up the stairwell in silence. Ashlie let them into the one-bed space and tossed her gym bag on the floor next to a haphazard pile of shoes and boots.

'I'll, um, I'll get that bag,' Ashlie mumbled, turning the living room light on and making for the door on her left.

'Just a moment, let's take a look at your shoulder first,' Kieran offered and reached out a hand to steer her towards the sofa, but the injury she'd mentioned flared as he gripped her upper arm.

'Ow, you bastard,' she grumbled as she let him sit her back down.

With horror, Kieran realised the point at which his hand had gripped her was bloodied.

'Ashlie, you probably need stitches,' he said quickly as he dropped onto one knee on the sofa next to her and tugged her sweater off.

She hissed through her teeth as the wool stuck to the wound peeled away.

'Do you have a first aid kit?'

'Above the kitchen sink,' she said from between gritted teeth.

Returning quickly, Kieran knelt next to her to tend to a very angry but thankfully not deep cut.

'We should call this in,' Ashlie sighed when he'd finished.

'You're right. I'll call Lorna while you pack that bag.'

'I certainly can't stay here now,' Ashlie agreed before heading for her bedroom.

By the time Kieran steered Ashlie into Kia's apartment, it was past midnight. There was no sign of Kia, and given how Lorna had reacted to the news, he was surprised his sister wasn't there either.

'Are you going to take me to bed now?' Ashlie asked, her voice soft as she swayed on the spot.

'Only if you think you'll fall over on the way there and concuss yourself.' Kieran fought a smirk. 'You didn't hit your head, did you?'

'No, but maybe you should stay with me just in case.'

'Uh huh,' Kieran muttered raising an eyebrow.

'It's too late to make up the couch, I promise I'll keep my hands to myself if we can just fall into the sheets.'

Chuckling to himself, Kieran tossed his jacket at the sofa, locked up behind them and gestured in the direction of his bedroom.

Ashlie led the way, putting her bag down at the foot of his bed and stripping down to her underwear, slinging her clothes over the duffle bag to be revisited in the morning.

She'd cleaned herself up in her own bathroom whilst gathering toiletries after their tumble on the street, but

Kieran was a bit grubby, so he left her to pick a side of the bed and headed for the bathroom.

When he returned, Ashlie was already asleep. Glad she'd found peace enough to drift off after the incident, he climbed under the covers beside her and let his eyes drift closed.

Within moments Ashlie had moved into the middle of the bed and as he started to turn to see if she was alright, she buried her face in his hair, her nose against his jaw as she cuddle-gripped his arm.

TWENTY-SIX

'When's your next shift?' Kieran asked over the round of toast he was buttering while Ashlie poured coffees.

'Not for a couple of days, thankfully. At least it's one of the safest places I could be.' Ashlie offered with a shrug.

'If I can't sit in, I'll make sure someone sees that you get there and back.' Kieran glanced over his shoulder to see her nodding.

'So, roomie, what do you want to do today? Or has your sister already given you a to-do list?'

'It's a vampire day for Lorna, she's turning in circles but they're oddly insistent that she stays on until proof of Hillary can be found. She's starting to think they know where the wayward Baxter is and are toying with her.'

'Well, that's just rude,' Ashlie huffed.

'Isn't it just?' Kieran smiled, 'She's thinking of getting Mia and Ben involved to free her up.'

'So fucking annoying that you have to use those two as a go-between.'

'Having our own rep has always been vetoed.'

'Let me guess, by vampires?'

'Most of the council, actually, we're too volatile.'

'Also rude.'

'It's true though, how often would you say you've had to call in a shift favour due to a vision?'

'Not as often as you think. I think they know who best to give them to.'

'Lucky you.'

'Do you ever think that it's all by design really?' Ashlie leaned a hip against the counter as she handed him a cup of coffee in exchange for the plate of toast he was holding out as he turned.

'Must be one hell of a headache for whatever being is dishing out jobs to whoever is best placed.'

'That's the magic of it I guess.'

Kieran watched Ashlie with interest as she sauntered past him to the dining table and took a seat next to the floor-to-ceiling glass wall.

He'd never thought of it that way, just that his family were shit on from a great height for reasons known only to Lucious if anyone at all.

'Where do you suppose Kia went?'

'Where do you think?' Kieran took the seat opposite her and raised both eyebrows.

Ashlie lowered the piece of toast she'd been about to take a bite out of.

'Maybe it's for the best that I have a couple of days off. She's going to spark some serious shit.'

'Only if she gets caught,' Kieran replied.

'Have you told Lorna?'

'No.'

'Don't you think you should?'

'Kia asked me not to.'

'That's your sister.' Ashlie gawped.

'My sister is itching for an excuse to disembowel Cain herself. If Kia angers him enough to make something of it, I doubt Lorna will sit back and take it.'

'Would Aiden let her?'

'Aiden doesn't control Lorna. He knows it, the rest of the pack probably knows it. She knows how to play nice when it suits her.' Kieran smirked.

'Just not when she thinks someone is taking advantage of her brother.' Ashlie arched an eyebrow.

'What you and I get up to is our business. She just wants me to settle down the way she has.'

'Who says you want what she has.' Ashlie shrugged.

'She knows I do.'

Ashlie swallowed a piece of toast as though it was rubble and turned her attention to the skyline outside.

They sat in silence to finish eating before Kieran stacked their plates and took them back to the kitchenette.

When he sat back down to finish his coffee, the shrill tone of the intercom interrupted any conversation that might have been about to start.

Getting back up, Kieran headed to the door to answer it.

'Kieran, it's Oakley, can you let me in?'

Checking the camera feed to confirm it was their packmate, Kieran pressed the door release immediately, seeing that someone was propped against Oakley's shoulder.

'Come on up,' Kieran said, mostly to let him know he had heard him.

'What's Oakley doing here?' Ashlie looked up from her perch as Kieran opened the door and kept watch for the elevator.

'He's got someone with him, he might need medical assistance.' Kieran glanced back at her.

'Ramsey's missing, right?'

'Yeah.'

They made eye contact for a beat too long, but the elevator pinged before it could get too awkward.

Oakley stumbled out from behind the sliding doors dragging Ramsey, who could barely stand, with him.

'Get in here, quick.' Kieran reached out to help him, lifting Ramsey by the knees as his husband caught his shoulders and they moved him to the sofa.

'Shit, what happened? Can I grab anything?' Ashlie jumped up.

'Two treacle-sweet cups of tea?' Oakley looked up at her, his eyes pleading. 'Or failing that, a couple of shots of tequila.'

'Let's start with the tea.' Ashlie nodded and scooted around the counter to set the kettle up. 'What happened?'

'He's been drugged, but I think he's OK,' Oakley choked back a sob as he stared down at Ramsey, barely conscious and covered in some kind of grime.

'OK, you might need to start in the middle somewhere. We know the beginning.'

'I only know what Kia told me.' Oakley shook his head. 'She sent me a message to tell me Ramsey was in a cab, that I'd need to meet it, that he wasn't in a good way, and to get to you for help. So, I just jumped in the cab with him and came straight here.'

'Did she say where she was or what was happening?'

'No, and further attempts to ask her have been rejected. Like she's blocked my number.'

Kieran glanced at Ashlie in concern as she pursed her lips and poured boiling water into two mugs.

'Did you ask the driver where he was picked up from?'

'Yeah, he said up in the northern quarter.'

'The hotel is up there,' Ashlie pointed out, needlessly.

'Do you think Kia went back in?' Oakley asked, panic in his voice as he sat back on his heels on the floor next to Ramsey and Kieran jumped up to collect his medical kit.

'If she found Ramsey in there, and she's dared to go back in it can only be for one of two reasons,' Ashlie said as Kieran reappeared.

'To finish this, or—'

'Or she found someone else,' Ashlie's voice was hollow as she stirred sugars into the teas.

'Let's bring Ramsey round and get that tea in him, maybe he'll be able to tell us something,' Kieran suggested, though they all knew that Ramsey had most likely been drugged.

'What are we going to do?' Oakley asked.

'What can we do?' Kieran returned.

'Go down there and kick his arse,' Ashlie snapped. Making Oakley and Kieran gawp at her. 'Oh come on! We know he's broken about a thousand rules and he's only hoping Aiden has more integrity than he does. Time to end this.'

'It's the retaliation . . .' Oakley started.

'So we start the fight!' Ashlie said, getting louder. 'And we make sure we do a half decent job of it. He was probably hoping to use Kia as a reason to throw the rules out of the window.'

'He probably just wants her out of the way,' Kieran offered.

'And what do you suppose out of the way really means?' Oakley pushed his face into Kieran's.

'Kieran, we need to move.' Ashlie shifted on the spot.

'OK.' Kieran nodded. 'Oakley, I'm going to give Ramsey a neutraliser, it could take up to half an hour to work, and even then he might just sleep. We'll head over to the hotel and raise some hell. When you feel up to it, whether you go out to MaryVaille or not, let Lorna know what's happened. Especially if Ramsey can remember anything, but the cab is proof enough that that's where he was. Let Aiden do what he will with that information.'

'What about Lorna?'

'I'll be in contact with Lorna,' Kieran muttered as he administered the neutraliser. 'She's not with Aiden today anyway. It will be up to her whether she heads out to the pack or adds to the chaos.'

TWENTY-SEVEN

'What I wouldn't give for a tranquiliser gun right about now,' Ashlie practically growled as she took in the trio of werewolves trying to look casual as they guarded the delivery yard.

'We don't need one.' Kieran grinned.

'How . . .'

'We get inventive.'

'I'm as inventive as I go right now.' Ashlie gestured to her glamoured appearance and coveralls, which had been the oddest but most appropriate thing she'd found in Kia's wardrobe. Given she was over half a foot taller than her best friend, she was glad to find Kia had sized up, whatever she'd needed it for.

Kieran had joked that it might have been Nick's but they both knew it wasn't that big.

They also couldn't morph like Kia could, but they had the ability to change their hair and eye colour. It wasn't a perfect disguise, but it would buy them time.

Turning his attention back on the three wolves Kieran began moving towards a van in the process of unloading vegetables into the kitchen bay. Casually, he took up a box and started helping with the unloading process.

Ashlie's eyes widened, but when he gave her an encouraging look, she joined in.

Keeping his attention on the guards, Kieran offloaded four boxes before everyone in the yard, with the exception of Ashlie and himself, started gasping for air as though they were choking.

Ashlie almost dropped the box she was carrying, but Kieran remained calm and collected, barely looking at the people around him as they sank to their knees and gradually lost consciousness.

'Have you just killed the whole department?' Ashlie hissed as he lifted one last box.

'No, just some mild suffocation, they'll all come round shortly. We should hurry.'

'They're going to wonder what happened.'

'*Smash the carbon monoxide alarm on your way past, will you? Follow me.*' Kieran set the box down and made a beeline for the kitchens.

'*Shouldn't we go in the way they were guarding?*'

'Too obvious,' Kieran hushed as Ashlie found the alarm and elbowed the safety glass.

'What if the alarms go off all through the building? Do you think we'll get a clear run at this?'

'We don't know where we're going, so define "clear run",' Kieran said, glancing back over his shoulder as bemused kitchen staff started to clear the space.

'Ramsey looked dirty, but not like he'd been splashed with whatever it was you said Danyl had been covered in, right?'

'No, that was some kind of corrosive.'

'So where is dirty, and big enough to have a vat of acid the size of a jacuzzi?' Ashlie glanced at Kieran.

'Basement? Boiler room?' Kieran met her gaze, then checked the signs at the next junction. 'Alright, we start there.'

'Man, it reeks down here.' Ashlie raised her arm to cover her nose against the acrid fumes wafting from the depths of the hotel to meet them.

'We must be getting close, the heat is only making the smell worse.'

'Yeah, but what the fuck is that?' Ashlie gasped, gagging slightly.

'Not sure we really want to know,' Kieran admitted but paused in a way that made Ashlie step back.

'What is it?'

'Lorna.' Kieran fished in his pocket and grabbed his phone. 'What's wrong?'

Ashlie waited, watching Kieran's face and preparing for the bad news she saw as his face dropped.

'I'll handle it,' he said darkly. 'Never you mind, I'll be with you as soon as possible.'

Hanging up on his sister he took a deep steadying breath.

'What's happened?'

'A courier delivered Kia's choker to Lorna at the Vampire Consulate.'

'No,' Ashlie shook her head in disbelief.

'It gets worse. Cain messaged Lorna himself as soon as it was delivered with a countdown. They have until tomorrow morning.'

'Does that mean . . . ? Kieran he can't have . . .' Ashlie began to hyperventilate, her eyes welling with tears.

Kieran pulled her in close. 'Apparently, he has threatened to send pictures of more bodies to Aiden. I'm going to see if I can find proof of those bodies. You . . .' he paused to take a breath for courage. 'You're going to make a run for the pack house.'

'You're sending me into the fight?'

'I'm sending you to the only place I know with a panic room.' Kieran placed his hands on her shoulders and levered her back far enough that he could look into her eyes. 'It's there or the headquarters?'

Ashlie nodded, weighing up her options. 'If I get that far?'

'Don't say that.' Kieran gave her a little shake.

'I'm not here for a long time Kieran, haven't you noticed? I'm only here for a good time.' Ashlie smiled at him sadly. 'And I'm incredibly thankful for our "good times".'

'Is that the real reason you don't date?'

'I'm clumsy enough as it is, being a guardian shortens my life span exponentially.'

'But I'm also a guardian, and a medic. I can put you back together again,' Kieran whispered as he ran his thumbs over her shoulders.

'Come on, you've lost love before, I won't put you through that a second time. I never planned to put anyone through that.'

'To use one of my sister's favourite entities, I think Fate might have had other ideas.'

'Be serious for a moment please?' Ashlie tried to calm herself down long enough to smile.

'I am being serious, if you walk away from me again, I lose either way.' Kieran sighed.

'You just told me to leave,' Ashlie spluttered a laugh to prevent from crying.

'You know what I mean.' Kieran smiled.

'Yes,' Ashlie admitted.

'So?'

'Ask me again in eighteen hours.'

Reaching out before he could process her words, Ashlie swept her arms around his neck and crushed her lips to his, but was gone before he could draw her in closer.

'Be safe,' Kieran muttered as she headed back out the way they'd come in.

Putting himself on high alert, knowing there were more bodies to be found and not wanting to become one of them, Kieran ventured down to the boiler room.

The roar of the furnace was his guide once the smell became too intense.

When he found the right room, he wasn't surprised to find it locked, though he was even less surprised by the flimsy padlock he could simply command open.

Pocketing the padlock, less concerned by them knowing he had broken in than being locked in, he slipped inside the door before having to stop and take a moment.

The smell inside the cavernous but poorly lit room, combined with the heat from the boiler, was suffocating. Kieran tried to ignore the large vat in the corner full of hell only knew what as he ventured forward, though he could guess. He could already feel the dirt Ramsey had been covered in seeping onto his skin, the grime seemed to ooze from every surface.

While he regulated his breathing to prevent himself gagging on the fumes, Kieran scanned the floor and any surfaces for signs of life or death.

Tarpaulin lay stained on the ground by the vat in the corner. He could guess what that had been used for. But aside from that, the only other thing down there was a few boxes and crates.

He'd come back to those if he needed to.

Moving slowly, Kieran moved around the furnace to see what was on the other side.

And came to a dead stop.

Three heaps of clothing lay partitioned off from the rest of the room behind chained fencing.

What had once been a storage area had been turned into a cage.

Frozen in place, Kieran let his eyes scan the scene so that he could work out what he was looking at. Bodies, the clothed bodies were piled two on the right, one on the left.

'Don't stand there gawping all day, that's how the last one got herself shot.'

Had the voice been any clearer over the roar of the boiler, Kieran might have leapt back at the sound, instead the rasping of a woman's voice had him stepping towards the body on the left.

'I might be half starved, but I've never touched guardian blood myself. I'm not a fan of poisoning myself, Kieran, so get in here and do something about this mess.'

At the mention of his name, Kieran's eyebrows flew skywards and his brain finally registered the voice.

Venturing towards the lock, Kieran stared at the waif-like creature peering back at him helplessly from beneath a muddle of tarp and blankets.

That a werewolf had bothered to grant a vampire blankets was interesting.

'Why'd they keep you alive?' Kieran asked her as he disengaged another set of padlocks.

'If you grant me my freedom, I'll find out for you,' Hillary hissed. 'But it would seem I'm still a pawn in someone else's game.'

Kieran's eyes narrowed, remembering what Lorna had said about Hillary and her recent findings. 'How the hell are they keeping you hidden . . . that's what the blood-letting is for. Cover up.'

'You guys catch on fast I see.'

'Shit. Lorna.'

'And you thought my brother was nuts.' Hillary rolled her eyes. 'Wait, she lived through that?'

'Long story,' Kieran admitted. 'Do you have the strength to escape?' Kieran glanced over at the other two bodies, wanting and dreading checking on them in equal measure.

'I watched the dark-haired girl sneak a werewolf away, I'm sure I can make it if she did.' Hillary looked in the direction of the other two. 'Stupid girl shouldn't have come back.'

Kieran sucked in a breath.

'They've been drugging the eyeballs out of that guy. Something about keeping him from being found. 'I heard them say they'd given him enough to kill an elephant on more than one occasion, but the poor bastard only died just before she got back. Then wham, they shot her before she could work out what had happened.'

'Why tell me this?' Kieran peered down at Hillary, only then realising she hadn't made to escape around him because she was manacled to something.

'Because there's nothing you can do for them, you should leave too.'

'Do you want . . .?'

'No, I don't want your fucking help, I just want you to free me,' Hillary snapped. 'I'll make it worth your while. If you get out of here with your life. They're more inclined to kill you than me it seems.'

Her eyes were wide with fury as she watched him tentatively track the source of the manacles and release them one by one.

'No rush or anything,' she said on an exasperated sigh when she was finally released of the chains and wriggled into a sitting position. 'But thank you.'

TWENTY-EIGHT

Watching Hillary drag herself to her feet without being able to help her was surprisingly difficult for Kieran. He had studied all supernatural creatures as part of his training, and they had all sorts working around HQ.

Despite the history with the Baxter clan and her refusal of help, it still felt unnatural to stand back as she hobbled away hissing, spitting and cursing a variety of names as she went.

He waited until she was out of sight before he approached the other two bodies. Bodies he was certain belonged to Nick and Kia.

Unlike Hillary, they were fully covered with a variety of material; tarp, hessian crate linings, dirty blankets.

Tentatively, he reached for the taller pile first. He wasn't ready to see either of them, but had to start somewhere.

As he peeled back some of the sheets covering Nick's head, he realised why they had used so many.

The smell was horrendous.

He was still clothed in the black shirt and trousers from the night of the explosion, but the colour had been bleached out of them. His once shaggy hair sprouted across his head in tufts and Kieran realised with horror that they must have thrown him in the acid at some point.

A scowl of confusion tugged at his features, that alone should have killed the angeling. Or at least seriously disfigured him. But aside from the hair and clothing, he seemed intact.

The smell, now he had visual, could be explained by that, a mixture of chemically rotten clothing, sweat, and what was probably urine.

'They really were torturing you,' Kieran offered Nick a mumbled apology and reached for the body by his side.

Ripping the sheet back before nerves could get the better of him, Kieran took one look at the bullet wound in Kia's temple and stumbled backwards to vomit in the corner.

Vomit he almost fell in when Kia sucked in a lungful of air and sat up.

'Fuck,' he yelled as he caught himself.

'Kieran?' Kia looked confused. 'What happened?'

He'd like to know that himself. He'd fallen back so fast, perhaps he'd missed that it was just a flesh wound.

'I thought you were dead.'

'I think I was.' Kia reached up and prodded at her temple.

What was left in Kieran's stomach threatened to join the rest on the floor when she squeezed a bullet from her skin like popping a pimple.

Taking a look at the offending item for herself, Kia threw it at the furnace with a shriek.

'What's going on?' Kieran ventured forward, but Kia had spotted Nick next to her and was blinking in disbelief at his face.

'He *was* here? All along, he was here?!' Kia choked on a sob as tears formed in her eyes.

Twisting, she threw herself on his chest and began checking for a pulse.

Kieran winced when she lifted one of his eyelids, expecting to see hollow sockets, but his brain tripped again when they both found themselves looking at, largely dilated, but eyes of perfect aquamarine.

Beating her fist against Nick's shoulder, Kia roared.

'How could you?! How could you leave me here to deal with this shit without you?' she whimpered. 'You asshole.'

'Kia, that's the second time you should have died.'

'How long do you think he's been dead? How long has he been stopping me from passing on?' Kia mumbled onto Nick's chest.

'I have it on sketchy authority that he only died a few hours ago.' Kieran tentatively moved to her side. 'Apparently, they were drugging him to keep him off your radar. Given the state of his hair and clothes, I'd say they tried to give him an acid bath too.'

'What?' Kia sat up to get a better look. 'Oh, look what they did to his hair, he'd be so pissed.'

Reaching out she twisted one of the tufts into a spike.

'We need to get you both out of here.' Kieran glanced over his shoulder, wondering how he still hadn't been discovered.

'Yes, we'll take you home,' Kia whispered as she continued to play with Nick's hair.

'I'll carry him,' Kieran offered. 'How are you feeling?'

Kia opened her mouth to offer Kieran a sarcastic answer, but instead screamed when, with a ghostly groan, Nick started breathing again.

'What the fuck is going on?!' Kia yelled.

'Shh,' Kieran hushed. 'We'll never work it out if they find us.'

'They think we're dead, they're not coming back down here, except to burn our bodies at some point.' Kia rolled her eyes in the direction of the furnace as she got a grip on herself. Getting angry at Kieran was a good distraction.

'Get Nick out of the way, I'll burn the sheets and stuff, so they think someone has already done it.'

'You get Nick out of the way, and I'll burn the sheets, you offered to carry him,' Kia bit out.

Watching her wobble to her feet, Kieran nodded. Finding a cleanish folded piece of tarpaulin and making sure it was big enough, Kieran set about wrapping Nick in it given his clothes looked set to disintegrate the moment they moved him.

'Why hasn't he woken up?' Kia was stood over Kieran's shoulder when he had finished securing the tarp.

'He's full of god-only-knows what.' Kieran met her eyes. 'Let's just get him somewhere safe and see if we can get some neutraliser in him.'

'We have the kit at the apartment.' Kia nodded. 'How are we going to get there?'

'Let's see if there's a truck in the loading bay we can borrow.' Kieran smirked.

TWENTY-NINE

Dumping the van they had "borrowed" from the hotel maintenance team three blocks from the registry, Kieran and Kia managed to bundle Nick in a cab the last six. They reasoned that if the van was discovered near the registry, that's where Cain would think they'd gone.

Entering the apartment building through the parking garage, they got Nick in via the elevator and Kieran carried him straight to the bathroom to lay him in the bath.

When Kia didn't follow him in, Kieran carried out a brief examination, peeling most of Nick's rotten clothes off with ease given they tore at the slightest tug.

When he'd finished a visual check, he went looking for his medi kit and Kia.

He found her looking terrified on the edge of the couch.

'He appears physically fine. I'm going to see if I can't flush out the toxins and get him to wake up,' Kieran said softly as he reached out to pull a strand of hair from her face, stuck to her cheek by tears.

Nodding as Kieran headed for the medical stash he kept in his room, Kia shuffled into the bathroom.

When he returned, he found her staring down at Nick as though she was unable to touch him. The lipstick mark on his chest, from the last time she'd seen him, was risen and blistered, the acid had burned it into his skin before the dead skin had flaked away leaving a kiss-shaped welt.

Reaching around her, Kieran stuck a needle in Nick's arm.

'What's that?'

'One of the strongest neutralisers on the planet. If that won't clear the drugs in his system, nothing will,' Kieran said as he stood back and reached behind him for a second hypodermic.

'OK, and what's that?' Kia raised an eyebrow.

'Relax, it's just a boost of vitamins and minerals. I doubt he's eaten since he went missing.'

'Since they took him,' Kia growled.

'Hmm,' Kieran hummed.

'What?' Kia dragged her eyes from Nick's prone form in the bath to Kieran's thoughtful stare.

'We can guess how they took Nick, he'd have been unconscious somewhere near a pack-owned restaurant,' Kieran started. 'But Hillary is another story.'

'Sorry, what?!' Kia's eyes widened. 'They had Hillary? Is she dead?'

'Yes, they did, and no, she's not.' Kieran slid his eyes her way. 'I let her go.'

'The hell?!'

'I had my reasons.'

'Why would Cain harbour a vamp?'

'The real question is who for.' Kieran placed his hands on his hips. 'Whoever it was for could be the one farming guardian blood.'

'Or buying it on the black market as a result. Desperate people can be bought,' Kia acknowledged with a nod.

'We have to get out to MaryVaille before Cain makes his move, are you OK to clean Nick up?'

'Yes. You'd better let Lorna know.' Kia looked pointedly to Kieran's pocket, he hadn't even noticed his phone, on vibrate, was ringing.

'I'll leave you to it, shout if you need a hand.' Kieran retrieved his phone as he moved, pulling the bathroom door mostly closed behind him. 'Have you got Ashlie?'

'Hello to you too, yes, she's here.' Lorna's tone eased as she spoke. 'Have you seen Kia and Nick?'

'Yes—'

'So have we.'

'What do you mean?'

'He sent the photos directly to Acheron. Kieran this place is in turmoil. What happened?'

'It's hard to explain, actually.' Kieran sought for the right words, hoping Lorna would twin him for the images in his own head.

'OH,' she breathed. 'Oh, really?'

'Yeah. I really can't explain because I don't know. It's up to you if you tell anyone, but we'll be there.'

'Right,' Lorna sounded on the brink of tears. 'Yes, bring them home.'

By the time Kieran had finished speaking with Lorna, Kia had filled the bath around Nick after getting the rest of his clothes off, and was washing the grime off him.

'Kieran?'

'Yeah?' He hovered by the door.

'Can you grab me some of his clothes, please?'

Retrieving an arm-full from the bedroom, Kieran dutifully passed them through the door.

'Do you need any help?'

'I've got him decent, but yes,' Kia replied.

'Is your car in the garage?' Kieran asked as they dressed Nick between them and moved him to the bedroom so he could sleep it off.

'Yeah, I think so.'

'Think so?'

'I've been all over the place the last few days.' Kia narrowed her eyes back at him as she began rummaging in her side of the closet. 'While we wait for him to stir, I'll clean myself up and change. Do you want to do the same before we make a break for the pack house?'

'Yeah, I should.' Kieran indiscreetly sniffed at the shoulder of his own shirt. 'I'll drive and you two hide in the back, if we're being watched they'll think I've snatched your bodies.'

'If they monitored my movements as well as Jamie did, they'll already know.'

'Let's hope Jamie was the brains of that operation then.'

Kia nodded in agreement and headed for the bathroom.

When she switched with Kieran they did a quick check on Nick and found he'd rolled onto his stomach in his sleep.

'That's progress at least.' Kieran offered Kia a smile before he left her with him.

Kieran offered Kia a smile before he left her with him while he showered and changed.

'Ready?' Kia asked, slipping a jacket on.

'Do you want to try to wake him again before we leave?'

Kia looked at the bedroom door. They'd tried twice already.

'One more for luck,' Kieran encouraged.

'Yeah, OK.' Kia looked uncertain but headed into the bedroom regardless.

Kieran placed his hands on his hips and waited.

When Nick roared, Kieran made a break for the bedroom, just as Nick made a break for the door.

On seeing Kieran, he roared again and headed for the set of windows by the dining table. Knowing those windows opened wide enough to jump out of, Kieran ran after him, but Nick roared again. Absolute fury poured off him in waves as he spread his wings and opened the window.

'Where are you going?' Kia panted, attempting to recompose herself.

'To end this,' Nick growled, his voice so gravelly it was barely recognisable

'You can't . . .' Kieran started, but Nick was already gone.

'Actually, he can,' Kia shrugged, walking over to the window.

'Aren't you going after him?'

'I probably should,' Kia sighed. 'Go back to the house, I'll see you there.'

Kia spread her own wings and followed Nick out into the night.

'Great.' Kieran said to himself before he started looking for any keys to any vehicles that might be in the parking garage.

THIRTY

Finding Kia's keys and Kia's car in the garage, Kieran drove himself out to MaryVaille as fast as traffic would allow. Lorna knew something was up, his phone was ringing constantly where he'd tossed it on the console.

'Where the hell have you been?' Lorna almost tore the passenger door off when Kieran pulled up to find several pack members leaving the house.

'What's happening?!'

'Evac,' Ashlie informed him as she jumped in the backseat. Kieran peered over his shoulder at her, thankful to have eyes on her whereabouts.

'We need to get down to the registry,' Lorna said as she got in the passenger seat.

'Where's Aiden?'

'He'll travel with Saracen, Davide and Acheron.'

'Is everyone evacuating?'

'No,' Lorna shot Ashlie an amused look, 'Most are staying behind to defend our territory, in case Cain sends any of his heavies over in Aiden's absence.' Lorna shook her head. 'It's got the panic room, and a number of safety systems, so it's just a precaution, but Aiden was worried about a land-grab attempt while we settle the legalities.'

Lorna threw a glance out of the windscreen at what had become her home as Kieran began turning the car around amidst the chaos.

'So, once again, what's happened?'

'Cain has reported a rogue angeling with fears for his safety. Ergo a breach of the treaty.' Ashlie rolled her eyes at him in the mirror.

'That was fast,' Kieran muttered. 'Considering he thought he'd killed the angeling.'

'Yeah, well, zombie Nick was trying to break down the door to Cain's private residence thirty minutes ago, so I think he's had to reassess his statement.' Ashlie couldn't help the grin that spread across her face. 'I take it there's also a zombie Kia.'

'Yeah, we have a pair of immortals on our side.' Kieran smirked. 'Once again, don't ask, they don't even know how.'

'Betting somewhere Lucious and Fate have had a fall out.' Ashlie held her grin when the twins turned to look at her before Kieran followed Saracen's SUV back down the drive.

'So where is Nick now?' Kieran asked, glad Ashlie was safely nestled in the seat behind him.

'Kia managed to get a grip on him and dragged him down to the registry herself. They'll meet us there.' Lorna glanced across the front seat. 'It's the registry who called us. Mia has also been informed given our involvement and is on her way down there.'

'What can Cain gain from any of this now?' Ashlie scowled.

'Nothing anymore, he's lost control of the angeling. That was his ace card.' Kieran shrugged, watching Saracen's taillights up ahead.

'He'll have a plan B though, you can bet your ass on that,' Ashlie huffed.

'He's had over twenty-five years to have a plan C and D,' Lorna agreed. 'The most I think he can do is disgrace the pack and have us put under surveillance by the registry while he regroups.'

'Who did you leave with Sookie?' Kieran was running a few scenarios through his head.

'Dante and Scott are there, Andrew was on his way.'

'OK, well that's a start.'

'She can hold her own too you know.'

'Sookie?' Kieran stole a glance at his sister. 'Oh, I don't doubt that. Where are the dragons?'

'With Mia.' Lorna smirked. 'And don't forget, the registry have their own dragons for when interrogations get sour.'

'They do?!' Ashlie leaned forward.

'Of course.' Lorna raised an eyebrow at Ashlie. 'Not that our fleabag will have taken that into consideration. He thinks he's above the rules because we broke them. Seems he's taken the we-do-it-ourselves werewolf code a little too literally.'

'What if he has?' Ashlie pushed further. 'You know, thought about it?'

'If he thinks he can get around a dragon, he's even more stupid than I give him credit for.' Lorna rolled her eyes.

When they arrived in in the lobby of the Registry Tower, they were immediately ushered to a corridor full of meeting rooms. Under guard by armed vampires, Cain and Sean sat on one side of the waiting room, Kia and Nick on the other.

Cain was looking at Nick with a cocktail of disbelief and annoyance, thinly veiled by the way his skin had lightened a couple of shades knowing he was a dead man if Nick was let go.

Kia was sat with her eyes closed. She didn't want to look at Cain for an instant, and keeping Nick seated was taking all her concentration.

Nick, sitting in a pair of sweatpants and a black t-shirt was barefoot, hair as dishevelled as Kieran had found him, despite having been washed. It was the crazed look in his eyes that had even the nearest guard watching his every move.

Given the drugs were still wearing off, Nick's eyes were bloodshot and the dark circles that had bloomed like bruises underneath made them appear sunken, which didn't help.

Aiden and Acheron held their resolve very well to see Nick alive. Lorna's eyes widened to see the state of him for herself and Ashlie gripped Kieran's hand to tell him she was pleased to see them.

He offered her a small smile.

'Shall we get this show on the road?' Mia appeared from a side room.

'What the hell have you got to do with any of this?' Cain spat.

'Councillor Sanderson is on the panel,' the dragon representative, Marie Silverton replied.

'For guardians. This is a werewolf issue.'

'And there is no werewolf council member.'

'She's not impartial.'

'The severity of your claims requires all council members to be present.'

'That's a point.' Mia turned to the Dragon councilwoman. 'The vampire representative isn't here yet.'

'Yes, he is.'

They all turned at the sound of a woman's voice and found Hillary dangling Declan like a worm on a hook from the talons of her left hand.

The guards retrained their weapons on Hillary, but lowered them almost as fast.

'Miss Baxter . . .' Marie started.

'Mrs Silverton,' Hillary replied.

'Put him down.'

'Sure.' Hillary threw Declan at Cain and the pair of them made a new doorway in the wall. 'I'd like both of these men placed under arrest.'

'On what grounds?' Marie scowled.

'Treason, murder, conspiracy to disrupt the city. I could go on.'

With a deep sigh, Marie turned to Mia. 'Get me more dragons.'

'Good idea, you're going to need them. This whole mess, well, it's all one big sordid family affair I'm afraid,' Hillary sighed as she placed her hands on her hips.

Hillary, having fed since she'd left Cain's dungeon, was looking healthier than ever. Though the twins had never seen her look quite so casual. Her usual leather or battle attire having been replaced by jeans and a hooded sweater.

The vampire still held the air of authority as she strolled over to where Cain and Declan were picking themselves up and grabbing Declan again, she slammed him hard into the marble flooring until he lost consciousness. No one even tried to stop her.

'What do you mean?' Lorna leant against a nearby pillar, expecting Hillary to mean her own parents.

'Oh, I actually don't mean you, though I guess we are family now?' Hillary looked up with a wry smile.

Lorna fought the urge to shudder. 'In a way, I suppose.'

'It's alright, I think you know I won't be leading the way my forefathers did.' Hillary waved it off. 'Anyway, I meant your new head guardian.'

Kia's eyes snapped open to find Hillary refocusing her attention on Cain, using her newfound strength to get hold of the werewolf and throw him back into his seat.

'Or at least her mother.' Hillary grabbed a fistful of Cain's hair and wrenched his head back. 'Who was sleeping with this fucker. And bankrolling that fucker.' Hillary tossed her hair in Declan's direction.

Kia's blood had turned to ice. The colour drained from her face.

Even Nick seemed to finally acknowledge reality and turn to her.

'Fuck.' Kia sat forward. 'Of course, the missing link was never a missing link, she was there at the heart of everything I was looking at. Through Declan she had a plan to topple Lorna, disrupt Aiden and get him a promotion. Through Cain she had a means to destroy the pack I called home. And when you stir it all together . . . wait, how did she use Casey?'

'That one is my fault.' Hillary met Kia's eye. 'I was seeing your brother, so when mine came back—'

'The final part of the puzzle clicked into place.' Lorna finished for her.

'Why didn't Declan kill you?' Kieran asked.

'To keep an eye on Lorna's whereabouts and an ear on what you lot knew, I presume.' Hillary shrugged. 'He made a lot of people *disappear* the night Casey exploded.'

'And I've been chasing leads around his filing system for months,' Lorna hissed.

'Can we prove any of this? Beyond dragon intervention?' Marie asked.

'Yes,' Kia said quietly. 'I have all of Jamie's files.'

'Where is he?' Hillary asked as evenly as she could.

'I don't know. He walked away. Left it all behind.' Kia shook her head apologetically but couldn't quite read Hillary, she wasn't sure whether the vampire wanted to rip her brother's head off or if there was something genuine between them. 'Knowing Jamie, he'll resurface when he thinks it's safe.'

'He thinks it's safe.' Jamie appeared out of nowhere and Kia almost fainted.

'I can't take much more of this.' Kia fisted her hands in her hair. 'What the fuck is going on?'

'He defected,' Marie looked Jamie up and down with clear distrust. 'He's been working for us as part of a plea deal. But will also need to become part of this investigation.'

Jamie nodded to the councilwoman.

Hillary let go of Cain's hair and straightened herself out. Jamie nodded at her, and Kia fought a smile, they'd be talking later.

'Like fuck you went all noble.' Kia threw a nod to her brother.

'Like fuck I wanted the city I call home completely destabilised when I knew it would be in good hands if our mother could just leave you to it.' He winked back at his little sister.

'We'll also be talking later,' Kia warned him just as Nick stood up and everyone started yelling over each other.

Five minutes later, Kieran and Ashlie found themselves alone except for maintenance who got to work repairing the walls Hillary had knocked down.

'Now what do we do?'

'Wait?' Kieran looked up and down the hall to the various rooms where several interrogations were happening.

With the number of people involved and the severity of the claims, they were looking set for the night.

'You two don't need to hang around.' Mia appeared with cups of coffee for each of them. 'If we need to call you in, it will be for witness statements only.'

'Shouldn't we just do that now?'

'All registry dragons are currently busy.'

'Wasn't Asha coming with you?'

'Asha and Luca went straight to another department to share everything they've already seen so that their statements can be cross-checked against everyone else's.' Mia shook her head, wringing her hands at her waist. 'I need to get back in there.'

'Is there anything we can do?' Ashlie asked as Mia turned.

'Asha and Luca should be released soon, if you're not called for statements by then, just take them, and yourselves, home.'

'Alright,' Kieran agreed and offered a salute with his coffee, grateful for any fuel. He was ravenous.

'You haven't eaten all day, have you?'

'My stomach is that loud?' Kieran smiled as he took a seat and Ashlie sat next to him.

'We left just after breakfast,' she reminded him.

'Did you get to eat?' Kieran looked at her.

'I ate with the pack.' Ashlie's smile was amused. 'There is always so much food in that house.'

'A lot of mouths to feed.'

'Think they'd let us move in permanently?'

'You're a pack member now, you're always welcome.' Kieran reminded her. 'Me, I'm actually family, so if you want live-in rights, you might just have to marry in.'

'Is that a fact?' Ashlie laughed, though for a change she wasn't outraged by his joke.

'It would help. Just saying.' Kieran's smile widened as he dodged an elbow to the ribs and took another mouthful of coffee.

THIRTY-ONE

When Kieran pulled up at MaryVaille for the second time, his cargo was slightly different. Ashlie had joined him in the front seat and Asha and Luca were in the back having insisted that they get taken back to the pack house for the night.

'Are they having a party?' Luca asked as he stepped out of the car.

Pausing to listen to the night air, they all looked towards the house and started running.

Bypassing the front door, they ran down the side of the house and out onto the rear terrace.

'Shit,' Ashlie hissed as they skidded to a stop to take stock.

'Well, Aiden wasn't wrong on this one,' Kieran stated. 'Let's get in there.'

Ashlie and Kieran threw shields up as Asha and Luca grabbed the nearest things to hand. Asha found a pitchfork, Luca pilfered a fence post so sturdy Kieran couldn't see how he'd manage swinging it.

'About time some extra hands showed up!' Dante yelled as Kieran blasted one of Cain's mutts out of his path with a ball of fire.

'How many?' Kieran returned.

'About forty, we've got Sookie keeping them out of the house, but it looks to me like they're going to try to smoke her out.' Dante nodded down the garden to where a group of wolves were using the chaos to get a bonfire going.

'On it!' Ashlie called as she zipped past, forming a large ball of water in the palm of her hands.

Within seconds the bonfire was a hissing ball of steam and Ashlie was using a telekinetic bomb to throw the werewolves responsible high enough in the air that several necks were snapped as they returned to earth.

Kieran paused his fighting to watch her in awe.

'Heads up!' Luca roared as he buried the fence post in the skull of a werewolf behind Kieran.

'Nice swing!' Kieran watched the brain that had been dislodged skid down the terrace steps.

'You don't hang around Nick and Kia without picking up a few tips.' Luca took a moment to look smug before joining Ashlie and dispatching any she hadn't killed outright.

By the time the rest of the pack were let go at the registry, the sky was showing signs of dawn and clean up at the house was already underway.

Kieran was using a power-washer to get blood off the terrace when Lorna and Aiden rounded the side of the house. Ashlie was burning the bodies of Cain's pack. Dante had been photographing and logging identifying details for the registry and everyone else was either on clean up or walking wounded.

'Miraculously, there were no casualties our side.' Dante placed a hand on Aiden's shoulder as Acheron brought Sookie out through the dining room. 'Kieran got here just in time.'

Oakley and Ramsey had taken it upon themselves to get a hot drink manufacturing line going in the kitchen, but when they heard Ramsey squeal in delight, they knew Kia and Nick were home.

As most of the pack ran inside to see them, Lorna wandered over to Kieran for a hug.

'Is it over?'

'Mostly.' She nodded. 'Declan is Hillary's to deal with, I'm not sure she'll be lenient.'

'She'll kill him?'

'Probably. She needs to show leadership to the vampires and dissuade anyone else from thinking of challenging her while she gets things settled.'

'And you?'

'I've offered to help. Working with her rather than against her seems to be something we're both open to. I've also been offered a position on the council.'

'Oh?'

'I turned it down. I've got the pack and Mia's got our backs, I've said I'll take Ben's place whenever the need arises though.'

'Interesting.' Kieran's brow furrowed.

'Could be.' Lorna's eyes lit up. 'As for the pack, the challenge was thrown out.'

'So, what happens to Cain?'

'He'll be incinerated as soon as they extract his head from the ceiling.' Kia grinned as she joined them on the terrace. 'Given the state he'd held the angeling in, they let angeling lore stand and so Nick got to decide Cain's fate.'

'His head was ripped from his body before the councilman had stopped talking.' Lorna's eyes slid to Nick as he appeared at Kia's side.

Nick offered a grunt, making Kieran's eyebrows lift.

'He's still finding it hard to talk,' Kia explained. 'I think we'll all sleep for a few days after this.'

'KIA!' Ashlie was suddenly in the middle of the group throwing her arms around her best friend.

'Hey Ash,' Kia breathed a sigh of relief.

'I wasn't about to let anything happen to her,' Kieran said, repeating his promise.

Ashlie turned to Kieran with a sheepish grin at Lorna.

'Don't look at me!' Lorna pushed her by the shoulder towards her brother. 'Tell him you fucking love him already.'

'Huh?' Kieran looked at Lorna who was grinning at him.

'Yeah, what?' Kia was also beaming, but in a knowing way.

'I fucking love you, OK?' Ashlie pouted at having had to be told what to do and then having to do it with an audience.

'And how long have you known this?' Kieran fought the smirk tugging at his mouth at the look on her face.

'Weeks!' Luca chimed in as he slid past them carrying a rubbish sack.

'I tell you I love you, you ask how long?! The fuck, Kieran?' Ashlie reached out and shoved at his chest, but he caught her hands to drag her closer.

'Of course I love you, you fucking tease.' Kieran lifted their hands to her face and drew her in for a kiss.

'Well, about fucking time,' Nick rasped as Kia leaned back into his arms.

'How does he know?' Kieran narrowed his eyes at Nick.

'She's fancied the pants off you for a while.' Kia rolled her eyes.

'But we met at . . .'

'C'mon, think about it.' Lorna rolled her eyes.

'Right.' Kieran laughed, his sister was technically famous, especially amongst guardians, everyone knew who he was.

'Just try not to burn the house down tonight, Ash.' Kia teased.

'What?' Lorna looked confused.

'When two guardians fall in love, it ignites more than a spark, shall we say?' Kia smirked.

'So that's what that was?!' Kieran's eyes darted to Kia then back to Ashlie.

'Oh,' Ashlie whispered, looking into his eyes. 'Apparently so.'

ACKNOWLEDGEMENTS

Thank you to anyone and everyone who completed this trilogy – you rock! I never thought this would have a final instalment so soon (that's a laugh since this journey started in 2014 – ahem 1997), but to close it off at a trilogy for now feels right. Onwards to new adventures, new characters and new romances!

Many thanks too to any of you who follow my journey on my socials, you'll have seen how much this book was up against it this year and I apologize for the wait (especially to friends and readers who have been waiting since 2016 to see how it all ended!).